Isbel Jordan

I will Have Revenge

by

S J Carvil

Gotham Books

30 N Gould St.
Ste. 20820, Sheridan, WY 82801
https://gothambooksinc.com/

Phone: 1 (307) 464-7800

© 2024 *Spencer Carvil*. All rights reserved.

No part of this book may be reproduced, stored in a retrieval system, or transmitted by any means without the written permission of the author.

Published by Gotham Books (May 23, 2024)

ISBN: 979-8-88775-939-5 (P)
ISBN: 979-8-88775-940-1 (E)

Because of the dynamic nature of the Internet, any web addresses or links contained in this book may have changed since publication and may no longer be valid.

The views expressed in this work are solely those of the author and do not necessarily reflect the views of the publisher, and the publisher hereby disclaims any responsibility for them.

CONTENTS

CHAPTER 1. DO YOU TRUST THEM?...1

CHAPTER 2. MUSSELBURGH. 12

CHAPTER 3. HEAD FOR THE HILLS...25

CHAPTER 4. I NEED TO WORK OUT..39

CHAPTER 5. TELLING THE TRUTH..48

CHAPTER 6. THE BIG GUNS. 60

CHAPTER 7. FORAGE INTO GLASGOW..69

CHAPTER 8. THE HUNT FOR JK..92

CHAPTER 9. KNOWING THE NAMES..113

CHAPTER 10. FIRST IN THE BAG...126

CHAPTER 11. SHE BAGGED A BRACE. 137

CHAPTER 12. REVENGE..145

CHAPTER 13. THAMES HOUSE...160

CHAPTER 14. A WOMAN'S SCORN..168

CHAPTER 15. CLOSING THE CASE..192

CHAPTER 16. HACIENDA GIRALDO..204

Chapter 1.

Do you trust them?

The constant thump, thump, as the speedball swung at a rapid repetitive pattern, side to side at a relentless pace with no sign of let up. Steve Blackman, the forty-year-old gym owner, stood there tight jawed, watching this six-foot-one Amazon of a girl giving it every ounce of her energy. His thoughts were if only one of these so-called fighters he had in training, could provide the same level of commitment as Isbel, he would have a world champion on his books. Steve knew all about Isbel, his concerns were of what was troubling her, for she had always been a workaholic, yet this was different. The volatile manner in the way the punches and kicks were being applied, meant that there was something very sinister going on in her mind.

Isbel's hair had been pulled together behind the back of her head, and kept in place, with an elastic band. What strands had fallen free, were now sticking to the sweat on her face, that was due to her continuous physical exertion's. There was always a meaning behind how Isbel trained, Steve knew this was no ordinary training work-out; what Steve Blackman was now witnessing. It looked as though; each piece of equipment was a person, where upon Isbel was invoking as much pain towards them.

Isbel (Isabel Jordan) twenty-four years of age. Her name, including that of her long jet-black hair, and piercing black brown eyes; that could burn holes through anybody's nerves of steel. Isbel's high cheekbones, were probably due to high levels of Estrogen? All these attributes, she had inherited from her Portuguese great-grandmother. Her lean frame disguised her strength, with her thirty-six-inch-long legs, and thirty-six C cup bust, that would turn many heads. Those that knew her, kept their distance, remembering how her impulsive, explosive rebukes could erupt; causing severe damage to those that had provoked her.

Alex McCallum the Lord Provost, (*Glasgow's Mayor*). Had introduce Isbel to Ted Blackman and his son Steve, in an attempt, to establishing in her, some controlled aggression. Isbel at fifteen had been before Alex McCallum, when he was a presiding judge at the court proceedings when Isbel, with three eighteen-year-old adult lads, were on trial accused of serious assault charges; all the lads ended up needing medical attention. He did not doubt that Isbel acted in self-defence, the injuries she had inflicted on them, was still something that had to be looked at seriously.

Alex McCallum, had met Ted Blackman, when Ted had first arrived in Glasgow. Ted had taken the position of a Juvenile Probation Officer. Alex and Ted's friendship had grown over those years. Alex had watched Ted's son, Steve grow and mature in that time, could see how much Steve had become, so like his father. Alex's respect he had for them both was why he asked them to take good care of Isbel.

Steve being much younger, at that time when Isbel was introduced to the Blackman's. Found that Isbel related more to Steve, then that of his father.

Those first early years, Steve had Isbel in training, they had not gone smoothly. Her idea of understanding rules and regulations, was where her problems initiated from.

This came from Isbel's earlier upbringing, making them acutely aware that she would not take fools lightly, was more likely, to hit first and ask questions later. This attitude gave reason to anyone that upset her, not to linger around for too long, knowing just how she would treat them.

Steve, kept a keen eye as he watched Isbel, at her work out; was certainly aware something was bothering her. As there was so much venom in her kicking, then with the cruel way Isbel was applying the punches, there was something that had her utmost attention. Steve liked Isbel, for in her way, she was honest, told it as it was, never fudged issues, always putting every ounce of effort behind whatever it deemed, that she believed had to be done. When he challenged Isbel in any way, she would respond, telling him how she saw the problem through her eyes. This automatically assisted Steve, who was always looking to finding the right solution for her, while he was guiding Isbel into her maturity.

Steve knew of his own problems, putting so much time into his sport he did not have time for girls. Then when purchasing the gym, again no time for romance, as it did not come in his reckoning of importance, Steve's mother Jean giving him little hints that one day being a grandmother to his children, would be nice. He had relied on his mother advise, when he was not, so sure that he was the right person being a male, to be a mentor for Isbel.

Steve answered the phone that was ringing in his office, though he still kept a keen eye on Isbel, with the various CCTV camera's that he had placed on the two floors of his gym. The ground floor was fitted out with;

Treadmills, Rowing machines and Bikes, and more equipment for circuit training. First floor for martial arts. Floor mats, light weights, punch bags and speedballs. As he has had more females taking up boxing, as a training regime to keep fit, he needed to show, that he ran a well organised set up. As he watched Isbel on the monitors, he wrote down the caller's name and number, with the date and time, in the phone's logbook, with a description of the nature of the call. All this time he kept gazing at Isbel. Steve had already noted the oversized t-shirt and shorts over her tights that did not compliment her figure. Knowing that was always Isbel's intention, not to give any reason for those around her to gawp at her. Steve waited for her to finish her workout, then time to allow her to shower and change.

Steve had purchased the premises in the centre of Glasgow when he was in his late-twenties. He had sat down one evening with his father to evaluate his life. He had been a promising amateur middleweight boxer. Then when turning Profesional, as he started to rise up the rankings. Realised that when he was challenged with the bigger, more competitive fights, had found himself a little bit lacking, with the weight of his punching ability. His father Ted had always supported him and had given him sound advice. 'Look, son; you have given it your best. You've made some money, so let see where is the best way forward from here?' They had talked about this part of his life when he was about to turn Professional and had planned to save as much as they could of the prize money, so if it did not work out, he had something to fall back on.

When he had been in training, he had used this same Gym; so, when it came up for sale, he and his father put together the finance into acquiring the business. It was hard at first, but gradually Steve built the business up and maintained a modern up to date Gym. And as the years rolled by, his reputation as a clean honest trainer, was soon recognised. Yet Steve had not found a top champion to put the icing on the top of his career.

Isbel opened the door, to exit the lady's changing rooms; found Steve sitting by the door. This was Steve's way to let Isbel know he wanted to talk.

'You got something to say, Steve?'

'Aye Isbel, like to step into the office for a second?'

Steve's office just had the bare essentials, a large oak table acting as a desk. An old HP desktop computer for his records and contacts; which also controlled the surveillance cameras. Two double metal filing cabinets, with many posters around the walls of various boxing and kickboxing exhibitions, including many photos of different big names in Boxing and Martial Arts. With only four chairs, his thinking was that his clients came to workout, not to waste time sitting in his office.

Closing the office door, Steve as usual was direct. 'I've known you for nine years now Isbel, seeing you thrash the stuffing out of that speedball, and the punch bag. Can only mean one thing, you have some nasty problem to sort out. As we have tackled some of your problems over the past years, let's take this one on together as well.'

Isbel reached into the inside pocket of her black leather bomber jacket, took out a folded A4 piece of paper; it was a Police report on how her twin brother Allister, had met his death. Passing the report to Steve, Isbel sat back down on the red plastic moulded seat, that was connected to a tubular metal frame, one of the four that Steve had in his office. Steve read through the Police Report, sitting opposite Isbel. His expression was as serious as to what was held in the report. 'That's not nice reading Isbel. Allister must have suffered through that amount of torture, to have died of a suspected heart failure. Did they, the Police give you any other information on what had happened?'

Isbel, had been clenching her jaw trying not to get emotional, not letting show, any sign of weakness. 'Steve, whoever did this to Allister, were trying to extract information from him. Apart from the extensive bruising of many heavy beatings, they had also stabbed him with a small bladed dirk, then inserted either a hot cigarette or some kind of hot poker, into the wounds. Twenty marks had been inflicted on him, and some of the bruising and burn scars, showed signs that this was over a period of three to four days. DCI Burke reckoned it was over a period of four days. As I believe, Burke had a hand in the torture, that should say was the actual length of time it lasted.' Isbel paused for a moment, knowing how Steve had handled other issues before, when she had found herself dealing with him. Knowing she could always trust him; yet she felt Steve's honesty, could also hold her back. That was not what she wanted, for to happen. 'Steve, Allister had been bound to a horizontal scaffold pole, he was suspended face down, hanging from his hands and feet, five feet from the ground completely naked. A bucket had been secured to his testicle's, which had been filled with water. That how a private security officer on his patrols, had found him, in some rat-infested disused garage.' Isbel's grimace that was etched on her face, showing her feelings of hatred, on whom had inflicted that punishment onto her brother.

Steve could feel the pent-up anger, that Isbel was showing him. Understood why, she had vented so much venom, at the punch bag and speedball 'Have the police said where it had happened?'

'No Burke doesn't want me anywhere near the crime scene, until he is sure forensics has combed the place. He is sifting through Allister's room at this moment, hoping he can find some clues to why this has happened, or detect if what they were trying to extract from Allister, is there. But at a guess, I would say it's one of those derelict buildings due for demolition, with the next stage of the Cities re-development programme.'

'You and Burke have a history. Do you trust him?'

'As far, as I can spit a house brick. He hangs about with that gangster Nick Diplock. Every Thursday night, when they play pool together. It's funny Steve, Diplock can play to a high standard of pool, yet he drops a packet to Burke every time they play. Burke doesn't know which end of the cue; he has to strike the balls with.'

Steve knew how Isbel felt about Burke, one of the lads that Isbel had hospitalised was Burke's son. Burke wanted Isbel serving time for it, had never forgiven Isbel. Alex McCallum the Lord Provost had seen what he believed, as the truth in the evidence. He had brought Ted and Steve in, to satisfy his belief that Isbel was more the victim than the villain. Even though the three lads each suffered severe injuries. The police reports gave Isbel as the perpetrator. There were many discrepancies, as much of the vital evidence had gone missing, in very mysterious circumstances, that did not favour Isbel's defence. Alex

McCallum had also given Steve a breakdown of Isbel's family history, of her parent's dysfunctional behaviour, with alcohol and drug abuse. Isbel with her strongminded attitude, not only defended herself, but Allister as well, from their parent's violent outrages. The consequences of her parent's earlier strained upbringing in the Gorbals area of Glasgow, which had its own code of conduct to be able to live there. An education you would not get, with any other form of life. Even when later the family were rehoused by Social Services, by moving them to the Drumchapel Estate, the new housing estate designed by Architect Sir Basil Spence, hoping it would help the family to turn their lives' around.

Steve was aware, that this is Glasgow, with its own unique kiss. Isbel having her own unique way, of giving hers to anyone who would foolishly try and take liberties with her.

'So, where are you staying, while Burke carries out his search?'

'I've checked into the Travel Lodge, Hill Street, it has parking.'

'And your job, will this affect it?'

'No, the team have just finished filming, I have been given some time off, before we are needed to work out the next stunt routines for a TV film.'

Steve had been instrumental in getting Isbel introduced to the American Todd Baker who runs a stunt team with his wife Erica, when they needed an extra female member. Isbel had taken to it, like a duck to water.

'Isbel if you need me, don't hesitate to ask?'

'Until we know what has happened Steve, I will sit on my hands; though I want the bastard who killed Allister to suffer, and I mean suffer.'

Steve was well aware of Isbel's capabilities. 'Don't do nothing silly Isbel, Burke has not forgiven you. He holds grudges the same as you do.'

'Aye Steve, I hear what you are saying.'

Steve, looking at Isbel as she leant back in her seat. She had heard him; it was more was she listening; for her eyes appeared half closed.

Isbel dissected what information she had, also with that what Steve had been saying to her. Steve and his father Ted, had become good friends, from those early formative years. Isbel had grown to respect them both. So, when she felt troubled in any way, they were the ones she had turned to for advice. Now here she was again taking Steve's guidance. Isbel was angry with herself, that she had been away on the film set, had not been there for Allister when he had needed her the most. Allister, had also been scarred by their parent's lousy upbringing in those terrible Gorbals tenement blocks. Moving to the newly built Drumchapel Estate did not improve matters, where the damage had already been done. Alcohol, then drugs, trying to hide from their mistakes, eventually killing any brain cells they processed.

Isbel thought back on how she had protected Allister; it was not because he was weak, far from it. Was Allister trying too hard to be big? That in itself could have been just as dangerous. Was this the reason why Allister had found himself in that position. Trying to be somebody bigger more powerful. Playing with fire, you can get burnt?

Isbel, made a move, she had made her mind up, with what she must do. 'Steve, I have to go. I will keep you informed of any changes.'

Isbel placed her card on the table, started to collect her bits together. 'Steve, that's the hotel, and the telephone number, so you can leave a message if needed. It's close to Stewart Street, so I can be on hand if the police have any new developments.'

Steve walked Isbel to the car park. She opened the rear side door and placed her bag on the back seat of the black Audi A3. 'Thanks, Steve, I was listening, and will be patient. I will wait to see what the police come up with. This stunt work has taught me to plan ahead, how to make things work properly. I'm going to Edinburgh tomorrow to see a mate of Allister's. I'm hoping he could throw some light on what Allister had been getting up to, since I have been away. I'll let you know how I get on.' Isbel reached forward and kissed Steve on the cheek.

'Bye Isbel, take care.' Steve was concerned, the tone in his voice, showed just that.

Steve stood and watched as Isbel drove off. He could see she was in control of herself, with the careful way she drove away from the gym and took care of entering into the flow of traffic. Steve knew Isbel's capabilities, he still felt that twinge of concern, though he was satisfied she would be alright; for it was those that did not know Isbel, that would trouble them the most.

Steve sitting in his office with the thoughts of how Isbel had reacted, showing him the Police report, picked up the phone and dialled Alex McCullum to ask his advice.

Steve, still with concern in his voice. 'Alex, knowing Isbel, she is not one to sit on her hands. Her and Burke have no respect for each other, I'm concerned that this could get out of hand. She is no wee Lassie, with how she has matured over the years, this has made her quite capable to give anybody a very nasty time, if she puts her mind to it. She is more in control of herself than she ever was; and that is what concerns me more.'

Alex McCullum sat back in his chair, the pensive look on his face showing how he too had concerns about Isbel. 'Steve your summary of Isbel's reaction, was of a tight controlled anger, this is a something we should be concerned about. For the report on Isbel, informs us that situations like these could fester, into Isbel performing a frenzy of uncontrolled violence. This was what Professor Davidson put in his profile of Isbel. When he looked into the possibility that she could have been involved with her father's death. This is why I wanted you and your father to help assist her. Which you have both done with good affect; though this with her brother; this could set off a fuse that will be hard to extinguish. There is nothing we can do Steve. Burke will use this against Isbel, for his own advantage; if he is not doing that at this very moment. The complaints I lodged against him, were looked into. His police record, was showing it to be unfounded. I had to leave it like that, I had no evidence against him, only my gut feelings.'

Chapter 2.

Musselburgh.

Isbel checked out of the Hotel and joined the morning traffic on the M8 out of Glasgow. The build-up of traffic was at a steady flow, with her thoughts on what she will find in Edinburgh had made her wear sensible office style clothes; black trousers and jacket, the white shirt blouse with only one button undone, flat heeled, black leather shoes. An official looking appearance. She wanted information and if that meant bending a few rules here and there, so be it. She had packed everything into her bags just in case she stayed longer than she expected to.

As the Baillieston Interchange showed up, on this overcast day, Isbel cleared her head to concentrate on the road, for this was the early morning rush to work for many. As soon as she had passed the Baillieston interchange on the A8, then when the traffic had settled to a normal pace, her thoughts drifted back to how she was going to handle this situation. Isbel wanted Steve out of the equation, knowing Steve and his father Ted would want for her only to let the police handle this problem. How could she, knowing the police were involved in this in the first place. The information she had given Steve, was so when Burke or Burns question him he would give them an honest reply, as he would not know where she would be.

A text started to come up on the dashboard display panel. Denny McKay was sending direction, Denny never used street names, only landmarks. He always remarked. 'Street names are never placed to read them, when you are driving.' Denny was an avid Rugby man and followed Scotland's national team whenever he could. 'Yae cannae miss the hous lass; it has the dark blue, of our rugby team, on the doors and windows.' He remarked last night on the phone. Over exaggerating the Scot in him, for he usually spoke BBC English, He had spent most of his youth growing up in Fort William. As he remarked the previous night on the phone, this was not his usual way of talking, though when he thinks about the national rugby team it becomes more prominent. Isbel liked the way he would use words to describe places when talking about Edinburgh, 'Auld Reekie, cheesin? Tis a shan, nae creasin matter lass.' Meaning Auld Reekie, like Ferguson's historical Poem. 'Old Smokey' Edinburgh. 'Cheesin' smelling off cat's piss. 'Shan' not fair. 'Creasin' laughing. The smile broadened on her face just thinking of how he would interpret his meaning to her, so she knew he was a real Scot. Then thinking of her own accent, how she had changed it, so to be able, to be understood by all the foreign nationals, she found herself working with on the film sets. Slowing down her speech, mouthing her words more deliberately, while watching her mouth move in a mirror. This had helped her to be understood. The way she spoke before, with that rapid-fire Glaswegian accent, nearly stopped Todd from letting Isbel join his growing band of stunt performers. The need to communicate was essential to be able to carry out the dangerous stunts, that they would perform.

First stop was Musselburgh Racecourse. The Satnav had beckoned her to take the A720 to the A1, onto the A6094 for Wallyford, then the A199. That will lead her to the Racecourse. Then she would pick up the landmarks that Denny had sent her, that directed Isbel to Denny's 1950's two-bedroom double fronted brick-built

Bungalow, with a single garage attached to the left side elevation.

Pulling up outside, getting out of the car. She stretches herself then adjusted her clothes, walked the short distance to Denny's front door. There was no bell, so Isbel tried the knocker on the letter plate, then waited. As the door opened, a medium build, middle-aged woman wearing dark glasses with long brown hair, that reached down to her shoulders with a gentle curl, that turned under at the ends. Wearing a floral wrap-around dress, that tied up to one side, showing off her hourglass figure, stood standing there. Isbel was in no doubt that the woman was blind.

'You must be Isbel, step in?'

Isbel heard Denny calling. 'I'm at the back Lottie.'

The outstretched hand of Lottie beckoned Isbel to shake it. 'Hi Lottie…I am Isbel.'

As Isbel stepped into the house, Lottie reached up and gently felt Isbel's face.

'Now I know what you look like Isbel, Denny has described you, as long black hair, and jet-black eyes.' Lottie proceeded on gently moving her hands over Isbel's body. 'Many people get a little uptight when I do this, but you do not object? That is nice to know that you trust me. I would say six-one?'

'Spot on Lottie. No, I have no objections, for I like to know who I'm talking too as well.'

Lottie turned and began to walk through the house to the rear kitchen diner. A modern fitted kitchen with every type of aid for Lottie to be able to work around, with her disability. All though blind, she walked as if she could see.

'Denny is in there.' Pointing to a door that read Private.

'Tea?'

Isbel did not need a second to answer. Oh, aye, please. I would love one, little milk, nae sugar.'

Denny's booming voice was heard. 'Come in Lass?'

Denny's room was an extension built at the external rear of the garage. The door had been cut through the external wall of the bungalow that led into the Kitchen. Isbel could see the full range of computer equipment, two large monitors, a rack for servers and printers stood out to Isbel.

'I've collated the information you gave me last night.' Denny pressed the print button, and one of the printers burst into life. Denny stood up, a mountain of a man six-three in stocking feet, with the girth of an old oak. His mop of sandy coloured hair with streaks of white, and his ruddy complexion, warmed Isbel towards him. 'Come here lass?'

His arms outstretched inviting a hug, Isbel duly obliged. The warmth from his hams of hands that Isbel felt on her back, always gave Isbel the feeling of warm hands, warm heart every time he ever greeted her.

'Nice to see you again Denny, it's been some time,'

'Aye, you can say that lass. You are more into films, I'm hearing?'

'Aye, Todd and Erica have acquired six more stunt personnel. Erica told me to sort out my problems. I've a month, then we have a TV epic to work on.'

'I see you have cleaned up your vocabulary.'

'Aye Denny, many of those I was working with, could not understand a word I said, so I took elocution lessons, now we are both the same as each other Denny.'

After Denny, had pulled the sheet of A4 out from the printer, he sat down. 'Pull up a chair, I've done some research. This is what Glasgow's Police have been working on. Three names have been put in their reports. Do they ring bells?'

Isbel checked the reports, then pulled from her pocket the report she had been given to her by Burke. 'See why I have to check these myself. These reports don't tally up.'

Denny nodded. 'To keep you quiet.'

'Aye, that's what I thought.' Isbel pulled from another inside pocket a postcard that she had protected within a plastic bag. 'This postcard from Allister to someone called Jake, was posted about a week before he died. It was in the mailbox when I arrived home. Why it was sent to our address is in need of an explanation? Especially the message that came with it. I'm here.

Denny put on some surgical latex gloves, then slipped the postcard from the bag, he placed the card into a scanner, then brought the image up on the screen. 'There are no irregularities on that side' Then turned the card over to see the picture side, a view of Edinburgh University now was upon the screen. Denny looked at it very carefully, then he captured the image into an Adobe photographic program, and passed some colour filters over the image. 'There can you see it?'

Leaning in closely to what Denny was doing, Isbel could make out some letters very faint but they were there. 'Aye, what can it be Denny?'

Denny tried some more techniques, but the first was the best. He printed out an enlarged copy, then placed it on a light board. With a pen, he traced over the letters, he could now see what had happened. 'When Allister had written the postcard, it was on top of a freshly written letter, the person signing the letter in a ballpoint pen, the ink had transferred to the card, as Allister pressed down hard, writing the card.' Denny placed the copy sheet into the scanner, then captured an image. Bringing up another program, he could now do a mirror image. There it was clear, 'Nick'.

Isbel knew Allister had been knocking about with some of Nick Diplock men. This proved nothing, but it did not say he was innocent of anything either.

Denny turned his chair to face Isbel. 'So, how do you want to handle this?'

'I've to find out where Allister had been staying in Edinburgh first, then who he has been going about with. When I came home, he was already dead, there was some mail, and six answerphone messages, three were from the same person calling himself Jake. I gather that could be the person the postcard was for. Two just hung up. The other waited on the line, said nothing. I dialled one-four-seven-one, but they had withheld their number. The rest of the mail, was junk mail. The funny thing is that all the calls were before he had died, nothing after.'

'Did Allister have a car, if not, how did he travel?'

'Nae, he didn't really need one Denny. Most of the time he used mine, but it was in the garage when I returned home. Denny, I checked the car it was clean, and that concerned me. Because Allister was not the tidiest of people, by any form of nature.'

Lottie had come into the room with their teas, and had stood there listening to what was being said. 'So, you believe whoever killed your brother had cleaned up after themselves. I gather you don't trust the police.' Lottie turned towards Denny. 'What if you check the reports on what Allister had on him when they found him, would that tell us anything?'

Denny opened the reports on his computer, while Isbel checked the copies they had printed earlier.

Isbel started to read aloud what was written in the report. 'This is it, taken from the crime scene by the forensic team. Clothes found at the crime scene: Plain white T-shirt, Wrangler denim trousers, white cotton underpants, black cotton socks and black Nike trainers. Left-hand trouser pocket loose change, value one pound, forty-eight pence. Train ticket, Edinburgh to Glasgow, Edinburgh bus ticket. Right-hand pocket empty. Back pockets empty.'

Denny stopped looking at the computer screen and turned his attention towards Isbel.

'So, no keys, no wallet. Did you let the police into your flat, or were they already there Isbel?'

Isbel sat silently racking her brain, searching for the events when she arrived home from the film set. Still thinking to herself; *She had entered the block of flats, checked her mailbox. Then collected her bags from where the Taxi driver had left them, in the entrance hall to the apartments. Entering the apartment which was situated two floors up. Was how she had expected it to look like, messy? Two months away from home with Allister living there. She paused, no; it was messy but not that messy. She started to look back at other times she had been away, and how she had found the flat then. Somebody else had been there. The phone calls none from the police. Burke had come to the flat with that moron of his sidekick, Tom Burns. The pair known to the locals as the Burke and Hare of Glasgow, the gruesome twosome. Then Isbel remembered Burke saying that he had the keys and could they search the flat for any clues, it could take some time, had she anywhere to go.*

'They had keys,' Isbel informed Denny of what took place on her return home.

Denny nodded, 'Then Allister must have travelled by train?' Started to work back on the timetable of the events that Allister probably would have taken before his untimely demise. His search for the CCTV coverage of the two Edinburgh train stations, Waverley and Haymarket, was more about how far back could he trace them was proving difficult. As it was over a three-week period, then after many attempts, he hit the right button, and had access, this footage took him back to almost the time Allister would have left the Edinburgh Waverley. Isbel's attention was now focused on that coverage, the platforms were packed with passengers. Denny asked Isbel for a photograph of Allister's then scanned it, putting it in a face recognition program, gradually they examined two days of footage, when the scan found a connection. Then just concentrating on that footage.

Isbel could see her brothers last moments; Isbel gave a deep sigh. Still watching the screen, a familiar face appeared watching Allister from the side of one of the green based pillars, he was talking on his phone. Isbel watched that person, who was watching the train leave the Station; he was informing someone of Allister's movements. Isbel pointed to a young lad in his late teens or early twenties. 'Can we get a copy of him, on my phone?'

'Do you know him?'

'I've met him, he was with Allister before I flew out for work. He came to the flat, and I made him tea.' Isbel again gritted her teeth thinking she could have been nice to someone, who could have sent her brother to his death. 'Allister called him Kenny, he might have said his full name, but I can't recall it. Though a few of Kenny's word meanings, taking into account the way he pronounced them, I would say Stirling.'

Denny taking Kenny's age put the known details into a search engine. 'Let's take it one stage at a time, keeping it simple.'

Lottie rose from the chair she was sitting on. She had been listening to what they were trying to do. 'Isbel, I've made up a bed for you, this is going to take some time to unravel. I've a Chicken in the oven any objections?'

'Nae, none. It all sounds great to me, Lottie. Thank you.'

As Lottie showed Isbel the layout of the house. 'Treat it, as home Isbel.'

When Isbel returned to Denny, he was still trying to gain access to Edinburgh's Police Records.

Denny could not believe what had come up in his search. 'Kenneth Simon Dalrymple missing person. He left home at fourteen.' Denny then reset his search with the full information. 'Let's see what this turns up.'

Lottie called them for dinner, during the dinner. Lottie asked Isbel, when she had first met Denny.

'Steve Blackman, who runs the gym where I worked out, told me that one of his clients was looking for a girl to join his Stunt team for some TV work. So, Steve set up a meeting for myself with Todd and Erica Baker. For two weeks, I trained with them until they were satisfied, I could meet their requirements. It was a TV epic about Scottish Clan history, that's where we first met.'

Isbel's thoughts, on her first introduction to Denny. 'Lottie, to meet someone that could be so big. For so long I had been looking down at people, then I could look up at someone. Denny knew I was new to this type of work; he took me under his wing. We became good friends.' Isbel again looked towards Denny. 'You were there as a researcher Denny, what you could do with a computer was magical. Then the first film I was working on. you turned up. We had some great times, we talked about so many things. Things that I had wished, I had a father who would have been there for myself. Just as you were Denny. I had never been able to talk about personal subjects, with any other person before. That you were telling me, not to get into the drinking, and the gambling culture, these film sets, can lure you into. I've never forgotten, I have not over-indulged with alcohol, only the odd glass at dinner, or ever even tried to gamble since then. You were the first person that showed they cared about me, without wanting anything in return. Your card you gave myself saying if ever I needed you, that's where I could find you, well here I am.'

Lottie smiled, the faint look of remembering etched across her face. 'Yes, I know what you mean about Denny, my first meeting with him. I was trying to cross the road. I had stopped by the roadside at a pedestrian crossing. Using my white stick to show I needed to cross. Hearing the cars stopping I began to cross. As I stepped out into the road a cyclist on a push bike crashed into me, Denny who was one of those had had stopped his car to let me cross, seeing what had happened, he came to my assistance; Driving me to the hospital. My injuries were not life-threatening, the doctor would not let me go home, Denny made sure I was taken care of. We were soon going out for walks, then to music concerts. We married six months later. I had started to depend on him.'

Lottie's mind drifted back to those first beautiful days when having someone there to help her. Losing her parents when a gas explosion demolished the family home and leaving her permanently blind and orphaned at the age of twelve. The years, getting over the injuries, then being trained to coup looking after herself. But it was the loneliness that was to her the worst part of living with blindness. The not knowing what was in front of her, tapping her stick trying to judge what the vibrations meant. Now a constant arm she could lean on, an orator to describe how the sky looked, to how green was the grass, with the fragrance of each flower smelt by plucking one, to let her feel and to smell its fragrance. How tall were the trees and how the leaves had changed colour as the seasons passed by?

Denny seeing Lottie's facial expressions, reached over and took hold of Lottie's hand. 'Best days of my life.'

Lottie's smile was genuine for it was the best thing that had ever happened to her. Going with Denny to hear the roar of the supporters when watching the rugby, was just as exciting to her, as it was for Denny watching the action. He would relay all what was happening, so she could live the moments with him. Having sight before being blind, Lottie knew what most things looked like, it was the jogging of the memory with the descriptions. Now it was the smells that were needed for her to recollect those images, that she carried in her memory cells, for it made life for her so meaningful. Walking in the parks, Lottie taking in those fragrancies, could now have an image in her mind of how the gardens looked, with what flowers were growing there.

Then Lottie still smiling with the memories of those idyllic moments. 'Why do you answer to Isbel, and not Isabel?'

Isbel did not expect that question from Lottie, the pause before answering was to do with her own recollections. 'It was Allister, when he was small could not pronounce Isabel, it always came out as Isbel, and it stuck with me. Mum got use to saying it, then the rest of the family followed suit. Even the teachers at school, it just happened to be how it was. Father Delaney tried to change it, even he had to give in, to the inevitable, for it was what it was. I'm glad it was not the name my dad called me by. Izzy. I hated that. My mother reckoned it was how I inherited my stare, when dad called me Izzy, I would just stare at him. till he turned his back on me, just to get away from it. That was something I found to my advantage; I would practise in my mirror to get it right.'

After dinner Denny resumed his search for Kenny, the Edinburgh police had two reports accounts of shoplifting, by a Kenneth Dalrymple, the first report gave no fixed address. The second a more recent report gave an Edinburgh address. Denny soon googled it and found it situated in the Portobello Area of Edinburgh, near the seafront.

Isbel noted the address. 'Let's hope, he is still there?'

Denny in his need for the right information made many more searches on Kenny, just too be sure he had got the right person.

Chapter 3.

Head for the hills.

Waking to a strange room, had no qualms for Isbel. Moving around on different film sets, she had become used to bed and breakfast type of accommodation. She used the shower that was in the bedroom to freshen herself up, then met Lottie in the kitchen.

'Morning Lottie.'

Lottie raised her head and smiled. 'Did you sleep well?'

'Yes, thank you, Lottie. The bed, it was just fine.'

'What would you like for breakfast?'

Isbel leant over to see what was cooking on the hob. 'The porridge looks good.'

Denny strolled in later, dropped his massive frame into the chair next to Lottie. 'I've checked the reports from Glasgow's Stewart Street. They are saying that drugs were found in your flat, are now trying to trace your whereabouts. They have checked the road traffic cameras, know you were heading for Edinburgh, yet somehow have lost you. So, I suggest you use my car, it is not what you would normally drive, but it is inconspicuous. I suggest we remove the SIM card from your phone. I've many here, so they cannot trace you'

Standing in front of the garage, that was connected to the side of the house. Isbel had to take a double look at

Denny's car, then back at Denny, then back at the car. 'How the bloody how do you get into it, Denny?' Isbel's, disbelieve in how Denny could manoeuvre his large frame into a little gold-coloured Nissan Micra. But how the hell he could get back out of it, utterly confounded her. Denny was right, she would be able to get around unnoticed.

Isbel parked the Audi in the garage. Then adjusted herself to the Micra. The Audi A3 was automatic, the Nissan Micra had a manual gear shift.

Keeping to the coast road it did not take long for Isbel to find the address, she parked the Micra a block away, near to the old fishermen's houses. This was at Newhaven, near Western Harbour, close by to the Lighthouse. Then as she surveyed the area. Isbel was just about to make her way across the road to the address, had to step back and wait. For the entrance door where Isbel was heading had opened. Kenny came out into the street, looked like he had just woken up, as he was wearing jeans, and a tight-fitting jumper, that he had just pulled over his head. This was by the way his mousy-coloured hair looked, uncombed and dishevelled. Isbel lingered back and kept her distances, followed Kenny. He did not go far, as he entered a local grocery store. Isbel checked where she could wait without being noticed.

Kenny was soon out carrying two pints of milk in a blue stopper top, plastic container. Isbel followed him back to his flat. As Kenny neared closer to his flat, Isbel increased her pace. As Kenny opened the door, Isbel was on him. Grabbing him by the scruff of his neck, and the seat of his pants, hurled him forward. The momentum, had him smashing his head against the door to his flat, which burst open on impact, with the milk carton splitting on impact, the milk flowed out all over the floor. Isbel had him under her control, closed both of the doors behind them. Turning back toward Kenny, he was just about to get to his feet when Isbel's right heel made contact to the centre of his chest, the impact splitting his sternum, this resulting in knocking him backwards. Kenny hitting the wall, slowly slid down, finished up, sitting on the floor, with his back against the wall. It had taken the breath out of him, now was finding it hard to breathe correctly with his now split sternum.

The stern looks on Isbel's face as she glared at Kenny. 'Did you not think there would be no comeback for what you did. Did you?'

Kenny looked at her in disbelieve, more from the force Allister's sister had just shown him. 'What have I, supposed to have done?' he stuttered between laboured breaths.

Isbel then showed the video clip of him on her phone, as Allister boarded the train. He looked shocked, at the fact that there was a video of him on the platform at Waverly.

'That phone call, cost Allister his life, so what have you to say? I suggest you take care what you say, for it is whether I take my revenge on you at this moment, or later?'

Kenny tried to move, but the pain in his chest restricted him. 'What do you want from me?'

'Who were you phoning, would be a start.'

Kenny remained silent.

Isbel unfolded her hand and started counting with her fingers, when her last finger counted ten, her heel stamped down hard into Kenny's groin. The pain he felt made him take another deep breath, which intern hurt his chest. He knew he was in trouble, that he was in no position to get out of. 'Okay...okay. It was Tom Burns, he asked me to contact him when Allister was leaving.'

Isbel had held her new phone close to Kenny, recorded everything he had said. 'Now is there any more you would like to tell me, that could save your arse, from me beating the life out of you?'

Kenny was aware that he had no choice, the pain he had in his chest was worse than the pain from his head, that too was not helping him. Even if he hadn't the pain, could he have had a chance to do anything?

Kenny had been thinking to himself, that he should have listened to Allister when he visited the flat, warning him not to upset his sister? She hits where it hurts, and can-do permeant damage. Even Tom Burns called her a wildcat bitch. But seeing Isbel at the flat, she was charming. So, had not taken any heed of their warnings.

'I'm just the errand boy, it gives me pocket money. Burns asked me to make friends with Allister, something about Allister running drugs for Nick Diplock. All the time we were together I did not see any proof of it. And that's the truth, because I do the drug run between Glasgow and Edinburgh. I needed to know if Allister was cutting me out, for if that was true, I would have been a liability, more likely been myself, ending up the same way as Allister.'

Isbel could see some truth in Kenny's words. 'I suggest you grab your goods and head for the hills. I'm looking for revenge, those that stand in my way will feel my vengeance.' She looked down at him. 'Phone.' Her out-stretched hand meant only one thing, and Kenny reached into his pocket, and gave his phone to her 'Have you another?' Kenny shook his head. 'For your sake, Kenny, do not try and contact any of them, you are alive because I needed information, if I need to see you again, you will end up needing long term health care.'

She left Kenny lying there, to reflect on what and how she had reacted. The drive back, Isbel did not want to bring any attention to herself, so allowing space, and by keeping to the speed of the traffic in front of her. When she arrived back at the house, Denny could see small spots of blood on her blouse.

'Is he still with us?'

'Oh, yeah, Kenny is still with us, but should be heading for the hills, if he has any sense. He won't get a second chance.'

Isbel showed Denny, Kenny's phone.

Denny's eyes lit up, as a leer of a smile etched on his face. 'Aye, now that's what I call treasure.'

Denny placed the phone, face up on his desk. Then from a sizeable instant coffee jar that held pens, pencils and various brushes, pulled a lady's large makeup duster, and very gently dusted the face of the phone, with a dusting of fine white powder covering the phone. Then brushed the powder off with the soft make-up brush, he switched the phone on. 'There 189, that's the numbers.'

Isbel could see the pattern of fingerprints fitting the numbers on the keypad. 'What's his birth year Denny?'

'1998.'

'That is so simple.' Isbel just smiled, how she thought, so hard to work out a passcode number she would not forget when she first purchased her smart phone.

Denny pressed the numbers in their sequence, the phone was now open. He pulled some cables from a small drawer to his left-hand side. Connect them to Kenny's, phone and to his own computer, then when prompted by the program, clicked save. This was the time to remove the sim card and the battery. The program sifted through the phone's memory, was showing there on the day and the right time the call Kenny had made to DS Tom Burns. 'So, he told you the truth. Now if you have Allister's contacts list, we would have the biggest oyster, with the largest pearl inside of it.'

Isbel sorted through her papers and gave Denny a list of known numbers she had, and to whom they belonged to.

Denny keyed those numbers into the program, that sorted out those who phoned Kenny in red, who Kenny had phoned, in blue. Then Denny allowed the program to sort out the calls to and from Kenny's Contact list. Five numbers had no identification. Denny didn't worry, he put them in another search program, eventually they too were up and running. Allister's calling list and how many calls Kenny had made to him, including Text messages. But none gave away what they had been doing together.

This annoyed Isbel for she wanted something more substantial, she was not contented to see little bits of gossip between them, for that to her was meaningless.

Then using the same program, Denny found where some of the phones were being used at this present time. Two were from Edinburgh's Royal Mile hotels. The G&V, and the Radisson. One in Sterling, was near Kenny's family home, the other two were in Glasgow, of a Miss J Nesmith. Isbel made a note of the phone numbers. Denny making sure of what they had, printed the list out.

Denny checking the list. 'Isbel, we need to see who these two numbers belong to, that are presiding at those two hotels, could you go and get visual contact and send me pictures of them?' clicking on the screen he brought up the Hotel security cameras. 'These cameras are never that good in visual quality, but we would have a clearer image from your phone, where I can get a better identity capture from the phone.'

Isbel did not take long to answer, she wanted to find out all there was to why Allister was murdered. If this is what she must do, then so be it.

'Aye Denny, I will keep in check with you when I enter the Hotels.'

Denny gave Isbel a new phone and made sure it was in his search program. 'This will allow you to move around undetected, it will also allow me to keep an eye on where you are, and with this Bluetooth ear piece, I can pass information to you, so you can locate who they could be. Then take a picture of them, I will be able to find out who they really are. Don't try and confront them, let's find out, to whom, and to what you are dealing with first.'

Isbel nodded; she knew it was sound advice. Isbel had realised since working for Todd and Erica, she had become more stable in her thinking. By slowing down her thinking reactions, she was able to respond more quickly, as it actually saved time. They had taught her to think things through, not to jump into trouble. 'You still need to be quick-witted; still knowing your limits as well.' Todd had been a US Navy Seal. Where Erica was Ex-CIA, both with lots of experience. Although Isbel had no fear, they had worked hard to show her how to control her impetus's impulses. It was the fight scenes, that was where she needed to be in control the most. Many of her colleagues already knew how Isbel hits people where it hurts, it was an animal instinct born from a very early age. Todd, having on more than one occasion, having to lecture Isbel for going off script. Her natural instinct of suddenly making unrehearsed moves resulting, in injuring some of the team.

Now Isbel needed to change her clothes if she was not to look out of place in two of the best hotels in Edinburgh's Royal Mile. Collecting her other suitcase from the Audi, there was a selection of mix and match clothes. She showered and dressed in loose-fitting black, silk and new wool trousers, with a soft silk, red loose-fitting blouse with three-quarter length sleeves, under a silk blue black jacket. Isbel restyled her hair, giving her more of a soft delicate look, yet not making her stand out too much. She needed to just blend in with the surroundings. The makeup applied to her face was again, just enough to achieve the same effect to blend in, not stand out.

Denny had kept a close inspection of the movements of the two phones, he was also trying to tap into them, if it works could keep Isbel away from being too close to the suspects. 'Isbel, don't park too close to the hotels, find a carpark. Just in case they have people around as security.'

Isbel re-took the coast road, found an on-road parking space that had no CCTV cameras in view. Walked a little way away from the Micra, then hailed a passing taxi. Denny informed her to go to the G&V first. As she stepped through the entrance to the Hotel, holding her phone to her ear. Isbel was already wearing the Bluetooth earpiece in her other ear; this gave her chance to hide her face if the occasion presented itself.

Now as Denny led her to the first contact, that he had keyed into the hotel security cameras. They showed only key places in the Hotel, he needed more detail from Isbel. 'Stop, look like you are concentrating on your conversation. Now turn to your left. Stop. Now turn back on yourself the suspect should be in front of you, hold your phone in front of you, look as if you don't believe what was being said from the phone. I'm going to ring their number, and you should have a clear view of them.' Isbel followed his instructions, could see a well-dressed middle age male, short dark-haired with a designer beard, his manner was of a strutting peacock someone who keeps himself well dressed, and in good shape. He answered his phone, but looked annoyed with the sorry wrong number excuse in a French accent. Isbel took three photos, turned and walked out of the Hotel, sending the photos to Denny.

Denny liked the images that were displayed on Isbel's phone, and had soon hacked into the next hotels security cameras, while Isbel walked to the Radisson and followed

Denny's instruction. This time the contact was an elderly woman, in her mid-sixties surrounded by many others. But Isbel's interest was on her only, again taking three photos she instantly turned and walked back out of the hotel. Isbel pondered on how it had all gone. But why did Kenny have contact with these two people? Isbel did not linger about, headed back to the Micra, then back to Musselburgh.

Later back at Denny's in Musselburgh. Isbel was relating to Denny's search results. 'There are no police records of these two people. But looking at those around them, now that what makes it interesting. Let's look at the first picture, the feller to the right of the subject with the shaven head. That's Jan Broch, Hamburg. The feller with the goatee beard to the left is Stefan Patras from a small hamlet called Javor in Slovenia. Interpol have a keen interest in both of these two. People smuggling, Drugs and anything that downright nasty. So, I have sent Interpol this information. Again, nothing on the woman but standing behind her is your old friend Burke.' Isbel was so interested in the woman who was on the phone, had not notice who was behind her. 'On the right of Burke, the feller with the neck brace, is Sam Bolter, an American lawyer for a well-known American Gangland family. I have sent their details to the FBI, and Interpol.'

Isbel started to look at Denny differently. 'You seem to be able to hack into anything and everything, yet not having to worry about it. Where most hackers hate to be recognised?'

'You have no idea what I use to do Isbel? I worked at the Doughnut, GCHQ. I was home on sick leave. My mother had just died, I was tiding up her estate when I met

Lottie, in six months I had fallen head over hills in love with her. Lottie knew how to navigate around here; she would have been lost where I lived. So, I resigned. With my expertise, they asked if I would still do certain specialist work for them. The servers link me to them. I took on research work for TV and film Companies, that is how we met. I researched your background, and found your reputation was unfounded, for your records show you have been almost a good girl, not as bad as others made you out to be. I know you will not hesitate, to take revenge on those who have wronged your brother, I do hope we could do this legally. So, I have Informed various people of what could be done to find the right answers, they believe that it could be of benefit to allow you to carry on as you are, with my assistance. You are not alone in this, for you have a good friend in Alex McCallum the Lord Provost. He has already been in contact with MI5 about you.'

Lottie touched Isbel hand. 'Denny had told me so much about you, even before I met you here, I liked the sound off you.'

'Thank you, Lottie, and you too Denny. I was so wrapped up in this I was missing the tree, that was hidden by the leaves. So, what you are saying that they know that Burke and Burns could be on the take, probably up to no good, as yet have no real evidence to prove it?'

'That's about it, in a nutshell, they have both covered their tracks very carefully. I'm still having contact with those in the intelligence at GCHQ, that have linked up with NCSC. Their full title National Cyber Security Centre, I've passed all the information to them that we have collected so far, we should have a visit from someone from the major crime task force. So, until then, let us sit tight and see what unfolds. You mentioned a Jake phoned; I have been onto that. A friend of mine at the department, that I worked in, has started to put Glasgow on his to-do list. He will collate all the files, of cases that Burke and Burns have worked on, will link that together with Nick Diplock. Even the finest pin in a haystack can be found with an extra big magnet.'

'Denny, why in Edinburgh, not Glasgow?'

'If I'm reading you right Isbel, I believe they are finding it easy to bring their illicit goods into Scotland. Glasgow and Edinburgh, these are the two Main cities that they can distribute their goods to the rest of Britain. There are other cities such as Aberdeen and Inverness, it looks as though they are here to set up their organisation. They have been using Norway and Iceland to travel to, doing their business between there and here. How Allister got caught up in this is anybody's guess.'

Isbel gave this a lot of thought. She was expecting just to kick some arse and smash the life out of whoever killed her brother. Now it has turned into something bigger, now with international criminals involved. Though she still wants to meet the person that made her brother suffer, for this was the driving force behind her need for revenge. Looking around at Denny's set up, this could be her salvation, telling herself to listen and learn.

The rest of the night, she sat with Denny going over the evidence they had uncovered. The ping that Denny's phone gave, told him a new text message had come in. He looked at the screen then pressed some keys on his keypad. The large monitor showed people at a meeting. Isbel now was understanding the importance the security people were taking, to what was happening in Scotland. The person in charge of the meeting, wanted Denny to give his account of what had occurred. Denny had it all under control, he kept his comments short but precise. The meeting was brief, everyone knew what had to be done. Denny aiming his warning to Isbel, 'See Isbel, they can see this is serious. Can you see what could happen if this takes hold unchecked? Your brother's death would be insignificant, to the lives it could eventually cost.'

Isbel's mind was not worried about anybody else's life, that was the Security People problem, not hers. It was now what she would be allowed to do, that really concerned her.

Later as Isbel laid on the bed, she was not looking at the plain furniture, with no sharp corner, or even how the fabric felt soft. She mauled through all that had transpired that day, the niggle that would not go away, were of those that had mistreated her brother Allister. Her mind could not let go of Burke and Burns involvement. Burke made the bullets, Burns fired them. The night had its demons, not allowing her rest from her thoughts. The morning light from dim to now a gentle light, still did not bother her, as she was still putting her thoughts through their paces. Isbel had come to a conclusion, she could go on trusting Denny, that to her was sensible, she could gain more information by doing so, though this was not settling her, she needed to do something to speed this up, as to what that may involve, was now her main concern. Heading to the shower to freshen herself, even when the water was cascading over her, she felt that the need to hurt someone at this moment in time, must be a severe hurt, not just a slap.

Sitting on the end of the bed drying her hair, Isbel had started to put things together. Her need to move this along, as she did not need this to drag on. Looking at her option, she must not use her car, as it is traceable; needs clothes that could change her appearance, making her look male, not female. Money, she needs cash, not credit or debit cards. With these thought's, a plan was gradually maturing.

Chapter 4.

I need to work out.

Lottie was preparing breakfast when Isbel entered the kitchen and standing by the kitchen table. 'Lottie, I need some clothes, if I have to keep out of sight.'

'What sort of clothes were you thinking of?'

'Hoody top, running gear, trainers that sort of thing.'

Lottie did not need time to think. 'Matalan, Seafield Way.'

Denny, hearing the conversation. 'Don't use your credit cards, they can be traced.'

Isbel just nodded. She did not want him to believe she had alternative ideas to his.

Denny had to be sure Isbel did no blow her cover, though most of the interest was in Edinburgh, there was still some interest in Glasgow that tied the two Cities together. If Isbel pokes about too much, the gangs would soon realise that they could be under surveillance. This in mind, Denny needed to know what Isbel was up too. Denny also knew if he were not honest with Isbel, she would go it alone, that would really throw the cat amongst the pigeons.

Denny reached into a side drawer, fumbled about till he found what he had been looking for. 'I've another phone for you, they won't be able to trace you on this one. But I will know where you are, hold the volume down for ten seconds, it would tell me if you are in trouble.' Denny was protecting Isbel; this was Denny being his usual self. Being an extra-extra-large person, he felt it was his duty to protect all his friends, his primary objective would be to keep Isbel alive, also to expose what these organisations were trying to achieve, at the same time. Knowing Isbel's patients will not hold on for too long, before it eventually explodes.

Breakfast over, Isbel still needed to move undetected. She damps her hair, then pulled it back and up, so it was tight to her head and none of it was hanging down. Wearing a baseball cap, she would keep her face covered from detection from CCTV cameras. With some clever foundation makeup, and no lipstick, managed to change her looks. These were the tips she had picked up from the makeup girls trying to make her look like the male double she was doing the stunt for, by darkening areas on the face could make the face look so different. Then checking herself in the mirror, to see if she could be recognised.

Isbel after giving them both a hug, then drove the Micra along the coast road into Edinburgh. Eventually driving into Matalan's carpark, Isbel had made sure to take notice of the CCTV security cameras, then choosing a parking place not too close, to the entrance of the store; if she delayed getting out of the car for a while, letting other cars to park, it would throw off someone that might be looking for her. In the store she preferred men's clothing, dark inconspicuous colours, giving a baggy look to hide her female frame. Isbel had put a lot of thought when packing, she had put some padding, to fit into the top garments to make her shoulders and back look larger, and flattern her breast, even special bum tighteners, she managed to put into her luggage. This was to disguise her female shape and make her look manlier. She had used this padding when dressing for the stunt parts of male actors; jumping of buildings, from trains and out of cars. Isbel having used aftershave of old spice, to give out the same message of manliness.

Lottie had given Isbel her old club card the one before she married Denny. This was to purchase her goods without anyone knowing who she was. Making sure when she left the store, to use her well-practised swagger walk, with her head looking down not providing a clear view of her face. Then Isbel returned to Musselburgh the same way as she had come.

When returning to the house, changed straight into the outfit she had bought, then went for a run around the Racecourse, nodding to any one that she passed as though she knew them, if any cameras were around, it would look as though she was a local out jogging. Isbel not wanting the clothes looking new, so she would blend in with the local surroundings. Isbel was soon into her stride, found the clothes slightly uncomfortable at first, but by the end of the run felt better as the clothes had loosened up.

After dinner, Isbel stayed in her room. The many street maps laid out in front of her were of Southern Scotland. She needed to get back into Glasgow un-noticed that would give her freedom of travel, next stage she phoned an old schoolmate of Allister's, with the phone Denny had supplied her with. At first, Hugh McKeon did not recognise Isbel voice, then when the penny dropped that she was, who she was, then he was all ears. After Isbel gave him a breakdown of what had happened

'So, a little nippy van, but not an eye-opener. And untraceable' Hugh paused for a moment. 'Yes, there is one, take me a week to clear it. Will that suit you?'

Hugh worked the car auctions and could pick up any type of vehicle, you just have to describe your needs.

'Thanks, Hugh, I will contact you in five days' time.'

The street plan of Glasgow was from an estate agent, showing commercial properties including lockup garages. Isbel had picked up the map that morning from an Estate Agent that had offices all over Scotland. Passing the Estate Agents office, she had noticed that a young girl, that was looking after the position was on her own, that gave Isbel the confidence to make inquiries. The young girl printed out many properties straight from the firm's online connections from their Glasgow office. Isbel noted various locations and properties that have stood empty for some period, also those that had a secluded location like lockup garages in residential out-skirted estates. Then looking online at any other properties that could be considered in her scheme. Her notes were now how will these properties, give her the time frame, she will need to keep her from being compromised in any way. Isbel using her memory of Glasgow, made notes on the map, where all the traffic cameras that were necessary to avoid, were situated. Now she needed to keep herself in shape, so her next search was for gyms. There were three gyms in the radius where she was staying. Then using google maps with 3D images, she could see what type of Gyms they were, she did not want one of those new hi-tech modern gyms. Much in keeping with Steve's gym, more for the martial arts. There was only one with that description, and she would check it out tomorrow.

***

Breakfast the next morning, had Isbel asking Denny how things were panning out with the security crime task team.

'They have established themselves in Edinburgh, and have someone in Glasgow.' Denny was so pleased Isbel allow them to do their job. His tone of voice and sincere plea for co-operation from her, was hoping it was not going to fall on deaf ears.

'Denny, I need to keep myself busy, so I have found a gym it's not far from here. So, will check it out today, it will keep me from getting in the way.'

Lottie's broad smile. 'You're never in the way Isbel, it's been like a breath of fresh air having you here. Denny has been like a big kid since you arrived.'

'That's nice to hear Lottie, this is not for me to be sitting on my hands, I would rather run naked through stinging nettles than just do nothing. I need to be involved, so that is why I need this gym, so I can kick the frustration out of my system.'

Denny reached across the table. 'Promise me Isbel, if you shoot off on your own. Let me know, so I can give you back up?' Denny did know about Isbel's fiery reputation, could see in her eyes that she was struggling not to let others do, what she came here to do herself, wanting to do it on her own terms. He had watched Isbel train with Todd and Erica on the film sets, where there were no holds, barred, Isbel matched them both, taking hits and returning them in the same way. This is why Todd like Isbel, it kept him sharp while improving Isbel at the same time.

The drive to the gym took Isbel ten minutes to achieve, mainly due to wanting to see if any traffic cameras were present, most of all was she being followed. The gym was situated out of town, in a rundown industrial estate, on the other side of the racecourse with plenty of parking. Once inside the gym, Isbel was pleasantly surprised, it was clean and well equipped.

Pete Leary, the owner of the gym, showed her around and offered her any assistance in whatever arts she was hoping to train in. The gym was well set up for boxing or kickboxing. Pete Leary studied Isbel to access her physic, soon had a good idea of her needs. 'I get a lot of young mums in the mornings, for both types of boxing to keep fit. Dropping the kids off at school then one to two hours of gym work, some treat it as a social club. More for the coffee and a chat. The lads in the afternoons, again in the evenings.' Showing Isbel, the changing rooms. 'My wife helps, Mags will be here shortly. So, if you are interested, you will have to sign in to cover my insurance.'

Isbel signed in with the false identity that Denny had given her, then apologised for paying in cash. 'Mislaid my card, waiting for a new one to arrive.' The sharp, whipper snapping voice of Magdalen Leary, sharp facial features matched her voice, that could be heard over the sounds of the mums that were entering the gym. Isbel changed and was soon into her training regime.

Mags and Pete looked on in awe, at the strict discipline that Isbel's training took on. The accuracy of her punching, to her high kicks, though it was the length of time she just kept up with a long lengthy workout, then with the skipping, it was relentless. Isbel was making sure she was ready for the task ahead. Afterwards, as Isbel showered, Mags sat there waiting to talk. Isbel came out of the shower drying her hair with a towel. 'You train as though you have a grudge against someone, need to talk?'

Isbel carried on drying herself, acting as if she did not need to talk. Then casually spoke. 'The job I do? I have to keep fit.' Isbel knew questions will need answers, had given herself those answers.

'So, what you do?' Mags's question, was no more than an enquiry

'I'm a personal bodyguard, for very rich personalities. Being female, I have to be that much more astute than the males.'

Mags had seen the Micra. 'So, it doesn't pay well?'

Isbel, expecting this type of questions. Then answered with an 'oh so what' attitude. 'Oh, the Micra, that's my brother-in-law's. My car is still in London I fly back in two-weeks.'

Mags Leary's casual look showed Isbel that she had excepted these answers. 'Time for a coffee?'

'Yeah, why not?'

Sitting with some of the mums, the banter of talk was about fun, sex, kids, then even more sex. Lazy husbands or boyfriends, the kids, and the TV soaps. Had Isbel laughing with them talking about life, no mention about money. They were all in the same boat there. Trying to paddle against a strong tide, didn't need reminding of it.

Isbel looking at what the girls paid Pete and Mags, showed they too knew the mum's financial plight.

The drive back, Isbel reflected on the morning, it had gone well. These were working-class people; who she knew too well, how they lived their lives. Bawdy, making as much fun they could, from the treadmill of their life existence. The reality of it, to sit and worry about life will only make it worse, so you try and laugh it off.

Later when sitting with Lottie, Isbel told her of her morning workout. The mums, Pete and Mags.

To Lottie, this was a different world than the one she knew, wanted more descriptions, so she could visualise this new world, she could not see. Denny listened in, said nothing, knowing full well how Lottie would feel her way through the stories, that he would tell her. Now Lottie had a different storyteller, with a different approach to relating to stories. Like a different singer with a different song. Lottie wanted to know more about Isbel, the need to hear her talk, with the way she spoke, would tell Lottie all that she wanted to know. Lottie's spare time was listening to audio books, sometimes Denny would select items that he knew Lottie would be interested in, from the newspapers; reading to her, cuddled up with his arm wrapped around her with the newspaper in front of them, as if they were both reading together.

'Denny told me about your jet-black hair, but what fascinated me more, was how he described your eyes. Who did you inherit those from?'

'Lottie, that would be my great-grandmother. My great-grandfather Malcolm Donald Jordan, when he was young, had just started working on the Puffer Boats. He had sailed down to Portugal, collecting Port and Sherry barrels for the distilleries. When one night while ashore he heard a disturbance. Found a local girl being maltreated, he stepped into helping her; soon found himself with a fiery young woman, whom he married when bringing her home to Glasgow. Isabela Martinez's. So, not just getting her looks, I also required her name.

Denny showed Isbel the information coming to him from various sources. The marks had been identified, and new targets that were coming into the equation had to be verified, from the database. Isbel, looking at the mug shots to allow her to know who, more to what she could be dealing with. As the evening set in, Isbel needed some fresh air, donned her tracksuit and headed for the race course. This was thinking time, putting the information that Denny had given her, trying to make sense of it all. In the report from Glasgow, the police were stepping up the search for her relating to the drugs found in the apartment. The way Mags Leary had spotted the Micra, she needed to protect Denny and Lottie.

Chapter 5.

Telling the truth.

The morning had an easterly cold damp feel to it, due to the brisk wind that was coming off the North Sea. The drive to the gym, Isbel rechecked how many CCTV cameras were showing on-route. Isbel, saw only one as she entered Craighall industrial estate. Parked the car then walked back to where the camera was situated on the side of a disused warehouse, checking where the cable led too. Keeping track of the wire, she could tell where the monitor would be. Checking doors and windows, she could see a broken window on the north elevation of the fifties red brick-built building. Now being able to look inside the building, it was empty. Isbel reached in and found the window catch was loose, she was soon shinning inside. Noticing the stairs to the offices, the dust that was laying around was quite thick, there were no signs of footprints. Telling her the building had not been used for some time. The cable entry into the building located, she followed the cable conduit down then it stopped, the cable had been cut. A quick survey to excess the buildings for its potentials, then hurried back to the gym.

Pete Leary was finishing the cleaning, getting ready for another day. When Isbel entered.

'Morning Pete'

Pete looked up. 'Need to talk to you.' As he put the cleaning tools away. 'Come let's have a coffee.' He put the kettle on and pulled two mugs from the wall cabinet, with a packet of digestive biscuits. 'Okay, who are you?'

Isbel did not try and duck the issue. 'Isabel Jordan'

Pete filled the mugs, then placed them on the table. Reached into his jacket pocket and pulled a police public notice sheet. 'It's saying you are wanted for information relating to drug dealing.' Before Isbel could reply, Mags strode in with some of the mums.

Mags had seen the Micra parked. 'So, what have you got to say for yourself.' Mags and the mums surrounded Isbel. Some had anger on their faces. Some just not so sure.

'I'm here because the two officers in charge of the inquiry into my brother's murder, are also connected to his murder. DCI Alex Burke and DS Tom Burns are in the pay of those dealing in drugs. I honestly do not know if my brother Allister is connected to the drugs. What I do know, is that Tom Burns had my brother followed on the day he disappeared. The person that reported him leaving Edinburgh, had reported back to Tom Burns.' The recorded message that Isbel had on her phone of Kenny confessing his involvement calmed the girls down.

'So why are they after you?' Pete was calm, the fact that Isbel had not tried to deny who she was, had told him to trust her.

'When I was fifteen, Burkes eighteen-year-old son, raped me. His two friends who assisted him all three ended up in hospital, and I was put on probation. Burke wanted me locked up.'

Mags Leary had her own mistrust of the police; for when she was in her early teens, she mixed with some dubious mates, who were into stealing cars and joyriding.

In one of the car chases by the police, the vehicle she was travelling in crashed, the lads ran off, but she was caught. The police said she was driving, that they had found drugs, but she knew they were lying. Her father made her join the Army to try and get her on the straight and narrow, it worked out for the best, but she still held a grudge against the police. Army life gave her the self-control she needed, now her life was in a much better position. 'So, why here Isbel?'

'I have a friend, the Micra belongs to him. He has a good connection with intelligence and is helping me to find the truth. He wants me to sit on my hands, I need to work my frustration out. Pete, do you know a Steve Blackman, runs a gym in Glasgow. Phone him.'

Pete Leary did not hesitate; he did not need to look up the number. After a couple of rings. 'Steve…Pete…Yeah, the lowdown on this police inquiry…Yeah, that one…She's good… Right mate, see yer.' He put the phone down. 'You've got good friends.' He nodded to Mags. 'So, you're good here.' Looking at the mums. 'She not here.' They all nodded.

A well-proportioned mum that could arm wrestles any man. 'So, what did you do to Burke's son?'

'I reshaped his face, with the belt buckle that he used to hold his trousers up. Then altered the shape of his nose, with the heel of my foot. He is not a pretty boy, and never more will be. What hurt my case, was that he lost an eye. I said that Burke's son did not care less about me. Burke twisted it to mean, that I said his son was careless losing his eye. Speaking for his son as character witness at the trial, because he lost an eye, which I would not admit fault, as I had counter-claimed that the assault, was of rape on myself, that I had acted in self-defence. One of the presiding Judges was Alex McCallum; who is now the provost. He asked Steve Blackman to help, and to give me lessons to control my aggression.'

Pete Leary, holding his chin with his left hand. 'So, what's your plan of action?'

'Rattle the birdcage, make some feather's flutter. Play one against the other, so they begin to doubt what the others are saying.'

'How are you going to that?' Mags's face showed a sense of eager interest.

'Make one of them disappear, so the others start to worry what is happening. I will need to get back into Glasgow to be able to do that. I learnt from an early age; you fight fire with fire.'

Mags listening. 'Seeing you hit those bags with your fist and feet, that's some fire you have there.'

Isbel had won them around, she did not want Denny and Lottie compromised in any way, with the Micra, it could have led the different fractions to their door. Now she needed to buckle down and train, for those she was about to challenge, were not going to lay down without a fight.

Pete kept a steady eye on her workouts and suggested a few ideas of his own. His connection with most of his client was through their military involvement, those still serving and those that just needed to keep in shape after leaving the services. He even helped to spar with Isbel, using Focus pads; also, with sessions on the mats, now and again would stop, to show her how to use specific positions for her own benefit. In a rest bite, he explained how in unarmed combat and being overhauled by several assailants. How to rigidly extend her body then relax the body. 'Keep repeating this, and you will have a chance to free yourself.' Mags and a couple of the mums, assisted him in the demonstration, Isbel could see it could be beneficial to have in her armoury.

Mags had met Pete when they were Instructors with the Army, then later met up again when they were with the Scottish Athletic Coaching Team, for the Commonwealth Games. They brought the gym when the previous owner retired and did not have to do a lot to make ends meet. With a flat above the gym, the evening sessions did not disrupt their family life. The mums were from the same school that their own children attended. When Mags noticed the mum's, were standing around talking about their problems. Mags suggested that she set up something for them to meet and have coffee, gradually the group became more prominent as family and friends joined them.

Isbel knew she needed more paper money, so after the gym session, she drove to Dunbar. Parking the Nissan Micra at the Victoria Road Car Park. Then walked to the High Street to a Branch of the Bank of Scotland. Isbel checking all the time for CCTV cameras. Making sure she had dropped enough hints to the Bank staff, that they understood she was travelling south on business. Now flushed with spending money, it was back to Musselburgh.

Later at Denny and Lottie's house, Isbel checked on any new developments. Denny seemed pleased how it was going. 'Burke is the go-between, yet we cannot establish if Nick Diplock has any connection with them. Our guy in Glasgow has put surveillance on all Diplock's main men, so as the operation intensifies, British intelligence are bringing in new team members to help out. Isbel, it turns out that the CIA has had people in Iceland, for some time. Now with the CIA involvement, this is giving us more help in tracking some of Diplock's known contacts. Which I have now been able to hack into some of them. There is no Jake amongst them, I know you believe he could be a key player, so we need to establish who he is? Now Edinburgh, lots happening there. Interpol and the FBI are jointly taking a keen interest into those villains activities. For this has turned out to be something new to the CIA, that these Crime Organisation are here, for they did not know they had left Iceland. British Intelligence had no idea how they entered Britain either, so they now assume that is how the drugs and illegals are entering the Country.' Denny then checked for any new emails. 'We have a new house guest Isbel, my old mate from the doughnut is staying to help.'

The yellowy blonde coloured hair and the red-blotchy face, bright blue eyes. Dressed in a soft check pattern flannel shirt, with dark brown corduroy trousers, looked the part of a computer geek from yesteryear, the only thing missing was a Fair-Isle tank top. His voice, thick but soft as he reached forward to shake Isbel's hand. 'Jim Anderson, nice to meet you, Isbel. Looks like I lost the toss, for I am sleeping on the couch.'

Isbel smiled. 'Nice to meet you Jim, knowing Lottie, it will be comfortable.'

Dinner was a happy affair as Denny and Jim mauled over past experiences. Jim in his late fifties was well educated at Winchester College, then Studied Computer Science at Oriel College, Oxford. He held all their attention with his tales of his youth. Isbel saw how Lottie loved this type of bragging that these men do. She may be blind, but not that blind to know how to read between the line, what was true and what was just exaggeration. Yet loved it anyway. When the ping of a new email was heard, Denny and Jim were there in a shot. Isbel followed to see what it could be. Pictures of six men entering a building.

Isbel thought she recognise one of the them, as he looked and acted like Tom Burns, a bit older with more colour to him. The building she did recognise. 'Denny that's where Allister was murdered, it's in the police report you showed me.'

Denny brought up the file, as Isbel had mentioned, it was the same building. An old rundown garage, in a derelict area of Glasgow waiting its turn for re-development. The police tapes still draped over the Crime scene. Denny replied to the email, Jim was trying to separate the men for identification.

Lottie touched Isbel's arm. 'Come, let's go and make coffee.'

Isbel sat at the kitchen table, seeing Burns entering where Allister had been tortured, made the anger inside her bubble up. Clenching her fists, she hit the table hard; once, twice, three times.

Lottie said nothing, allowing Isbel to let it out. Lottie had felt the same way many times before, when tripping over things, trying to come to term with her blindness.

Then gritted her teeth and got over it. Feeling Isbel's presence, she could sense her need to do something, yet she knew Isbel trusted Denny, was allowing him his involvement, yet for how long? Denny had told her of the way Isbel could react when provoked, now each revelation was shortening the fuse in Isbel, one spark will light that short fuse, then she will explode.

'Give them time Isbel, they may think they are safe, that is when they become careless.' Lottie reached out to her; Isbel took Lottie's hand in hers. Isbel's gentle grip, pleased Lottie, as she wanted to settle Isbel reaction to what was unsettling her.

The coffee was strong, as Isbel drank, she plotted. Lottie sensed the vibes that Isbel sent out. 'Have you a fella Isbel?'

These word's smacked at Isbel, brought her out from her thoughts. 'Have I fella? Nae, Nae, not at all…Nae?'

'What never?'

'Nae, never.'

'Do you prefer women?'

'Nae, Lottie, I have never thought about it. I have never been tempted, those fella's that were my age I thought were kids, the older men, they were there just trying to use me to their own advantage.'

Isbel's thoughts were now about her past life, how she looked after Allister. The paper-round Isbel maintained for the Patel's corner newsagents' shop, it paid her a few pounds, then helping in Mulvaney's grocer's shop gave her a bit more money, at first it helped to buy the essential things needed for her and Allister to survive. Her parents need to feed their drug addiction, meant food was not their priority. When her parents died, the work prospects got better as Isbel became older she could do more, finding that people began to rely on her. Then came the stunt work, that paid her well, allowing her to rent the apartment away from Drumchapel Estate, from the friends, that would get Allister into trouble, Isbel had bought second-hand furniture, Allister had no respect for how he treated things around him. She had told herself she would buy new when he showed more respect. Knowing Allister was no angel, though he was her brother. The purchase of a brand-new car, the apartment came with a garage. Was how Isbel encouraged Allister in the move.

It was then, that she felt Lottie holding her hand, with her spare hand she gently covered Lottie's hand.

'Thanks, Lottie, you are okay.'

Isbel pondered with her thoughts, looking back on what she had done the good, and the bad. The many regrets, if only she could undo some of them.

'Lottie, I know my past life has not been easy. Though I still try to do things that are deemed right…although it seemed that at the time, no one else did.'

Isbel thoughts were now thinking of her parents. 'Lottie, my first recollection of my parents, were of kind loving parents. Then things started to go wrong, Dad would find fault with everything, he started drinking, then smoking pot. Lager and pot don't mix, that turned him into a monster, mum followed suit, soon I had two monsters to put up with. Then when the drugs killed them, we moved in with my mum's parents. But they were old, and Allister was becoming a problem. One day…I'd had'…Isbel's thoughts made her pause for a moment… 'I had enough and took it out on him. He never questioned me again, whatever I said, went. No drinking, no drugs. He knew what to expect if he crossed that line. He was allowed most boyish things, but never them.'

'That's why you don't trust what has been said about him.'

'In a kind of away, yes. Though with my going away with the job, when the cats away, the mice will play. My nan would say, 'you are only, who you run around with.' So, I needed to know who he was running around with.' The slight softness in Isbel's voice was the regrets that going away, she had lost that contact she previously had with Allister.

Isbel's thoughts on her brother's attitudes rambled through her mind. 'He had been a man, not a boy…a boy! that's it.' Isbel started to giggle at herself not realising before, then seeing the puzzled look on Lottie's face 'Sorry Lottie, Jake is not male, but female. She attended the same school as Allister and myself. The deep voice is why she is called Jake, not Jacklyn. Yet she is some pretty girl, Allister always liked her. As I would look after him, he would look after her.' Isbel rose from the chair and went to inform Denny.

Denny was looking at the ID of a Gordon Burns the brother of Tom Burns. Isbel quickly read the report. 'So, it runs in the family? Denny, I know who Jake is. Jacklyn Kennedy, 24. She came from the same estate as Allister and myself, Drumchapel. Her deep manly voice is what threw us, as I always called her Jacklyn.'

Jim entered the details into his search program. And the monitor flashed many Jacklyn Kennedy's then stopped.

Isbel smiled. 'That's her.'

The results came from the passport office. Then Jim entered, Jake's last known entry or departure. 'Glasgow Airport. She left the same day as Allister died.'

Denny, looking for the video camera shots of that time, she would have gone through the security checks. 'There she is. Now, is she on her own?'

Isbel closed in to see Jacklyn's face. 'Denny, could you enlarge her face?' As the face became enlarged, Isbel could see the frightened look Jacklyn had, as her eyes darted about, wary if she was being seen. 'So, she knew what was happening.'

Jim Anderson had already checked the travel documents that Jacklyn had used, with the flight schedules. 'Malaga.' He also checked all the other passengers, to see if any were suspicious.

Denny passed the information to the security team that was handling this investigation. Then received the notice that Denny would have a visit from, CIA and FBI agents, and who they would be; sometime tomorrow.

The report that Isbel had drawn a large sum of money from The Bank of Scotland, in Dunbar. Had Burke and Burns studying every Traffic control camera they could.

And alerted every police force in the North East of England of their interest in apprehending Isabel Jordan for drug trafficking. Burke was so happy that Isbel was on the run this gave him the reason to pursue her, that she had something to hide. For this kept her out of his hair and allowed him and Tom to carry on with their involvements in Edinburgh. 'Tom we must keep this as professional as we can, we don't want any come backs, let's make sure all the evidence is laid at her door. This has already allowed us, an excuse to be in Edinburgh with our search for Isbel. But what I can't understand, is why we have not had any sightings of her?'

DC Tom Burns sitting on the corner edge of Burkes desk. 'It does not matter, when she raises her head, we have planted enough evidence to put her away. Gordon and Jose are staying in her flat, so if she shows up there, we can dispose of her in any way we want. You will get your revenge on her, for what she did to your son Robert.'

Chapter 6.

The Big Guns.

The drive in the morning to Craighall gym gave Isbel time to think. She needed all the information she could find, having an idea of what was actually happening could be the best way to find a way, how to make them show their hands.

Pete, Mags and the mums were already there waiting. This had brought some adventure into their lives, which they did not want to miss a single thing. Even to just watching Isbel workout was enough for them. for it made the day for them; as it took them away from their typical humdrum days; looking after their homes and their kids.

As Isbel upped the pace of her training, that's when Mags, finding the going was getting too hard, would back off, to allow Isbel and Pete to carry on. Even Pete would stop to take a breather, but not Isbel, she would step into another routine and up the pace. When Isbel finished, she sat with them all, drinking coffee and eating plain digestive biscuits. Listening to the mums talking about their men. Pete would slink off as he knew many of the men, the mums were talking about. He felt it was the best thing to do, so he could look their fellas in the eye without feeling awkward.

On the drive home, a scheme Isbel was putting into her head, started to become more evident. She knew she needed to put more time into her training, to get her energy levels up to full speed, so must not push herself into doing something rash, that could lead her into more trouble. She must be seen to be following their advice. As she approached the house, the large black Audi Q5 parked outside the house had the USofA, stamped all over it. Not in writing but with attitude, big and brash. Isbel did not need to know who it could be, as if it was written, in bright red flashing neon lights.

Lottie had been waiting by the window, for the familiar sound of the Micra's door closing. Then went and opened the door. 'We have visitors Isbel.'

As Isbel entered the lounge, the two agents stood up.

The first agent was a fortyish white American, with short dark hair, sporting a college boy hairstyle. Typical mid-American law officer, as his demeanour had that pulled back shoulders and straight backbone, with the usual straight face. Look at me attitude. Just like a gymnastic preparing for a run at a wooden horse. He stepped forward to shake Isbel's outstretched hand, 'FBI agent John Keats, nice to meet you, Miss Jordan.' He then stepped back and let the other agent introduce himself.

Afro-American, thick-set, in his mid-fifties. His face showed he was a no-nonsense type of person; he came over as, strictly to the Pentagon Bible. 'CIA agent Jesmond Freeman, it's my pleasure, Miss Jordan.' He paused for a moment, then went on to explain to Isbel why they were there. 'GCHQ has been updating us on this case, it is an International joint operation. The need to bring this group of criminals down, is for all our concerns, we have never known so many different international crime organisations, to be in this together all at the same time. We have been following leads for five years. Yet we have not discovered what it is they were trying to achieve. The people here are not the main Gang leaders, we believe that they are here, to getting this criminal operation up and running. This is frightening to think that different international gangland organisations, could be joining together all over the world. It would certainly make law enforcement, harder for us to react to?'

Denny, coming from his computer den, joined them. 'These are the results of the searches on those last faces, that the MI5 agent has uncovered. Once again not the top men but seconds in command.' Denny was placing the papers in front of them, so the two agents could see what he had. 'Gordon Burns is the key to the whole set up, when we sent the details to the Pentagon, at Fairfax, they had the same face to many names. Now they have his real name they will be able to track him better. I am in contact with Interpol, so we can combine our resources on this.'

Agent Freeman studied the print out that Denny had given him.

'Fairfax is at your disposal. A team from all the relevant departments have been set up to handle this, we believe that Gordon Burns has been in Colombia for several years with a drug cartel, but as yet we don't know which one. His face kept popping up and around the world but always with a different name.' Agent Freeman produced various alias that Gordon Burns had used. 'But every time we had a lead, he disappeared. Then in Iceland two years ago a body was found that had the same wounds as Isbel's brother, Allister was found with. Then by chance Interpol contacted us, they were looking for a suspect. That when we discover we were chasing the same man. Isbel, we believe Gordon Burns and his sidekick the Colombian, are one or both, connected with of your brother's murder.'

Agent Freeman gave Denny a list of all those that his department had already identified. 'These we do know off, yet not enough to pull them in for anything that would put them away for a lengthy time. allowing them to carry on hoping they would lead us to who were the big fish that was controlling the shoal. We know that only after they had departed from the scene, did we find out what problems they had left behind them.'

Isbel did not move; her brain was working overtime. Her plans were changing, she needed to revenge Allister. But being also angry with herself for not being there for him in his hour of need. She needed to heed Todd and Erica's warnings of don't let your emotion control you, but look at yourself as the dog that wagged its tail, not the dog being wagged, by its tail. She knew how easy it could be to lose the fight, if she lost her self-control. Now she needed to understand who was in the mix, like the other men who went into that garage with the Burns Brothers. The other question was why were they there? It was still a crime scene.

Denny was looking at the list that agent Freeman had given him, two of the faces were ringing bells, but the names didn't. Denny called for Jim.

Jim Anderson strolled in with a casual air about him. 'What's up Denny?' As Jim looked over Denny's shoulder.

'These two Jim, I have seen these faces before but cannot remember where.'

Jim took the list and studied it carefully, till it started to make sense. 'The Bristol drug ring, we had pictures but no names. The Drug Squad arrested ten members of the drug ring, not them two, our investigation established them two, as ex-IRA, that was all we had to go on. Can I get Bert Stubbs on this, he would love the challenge, with his knowledge of the IRA? Now with names to those faces, he will have something to sink his teeth into.'

Agent Freeman nodded his agreement. 'Yes, the more we know, the better we will be able to sort this mess out.'

Jim did not hesitate and was sending the info to Bert Stubbs at GCHQ.

Isbel went with him. She was more interested in those that were with the Burns brothers. Sitting down in Denny's computer den, 'Jim, does any of those on that list relate to those that entered the garage where Allister died?'

Jim put up the video on the monitor, that showed the group entering the garage. 'That one there Isbel, can you see his limp. That's Kieron McCreary we have had information on him, the last sighting of him was in Libya. Now he is here, what we tried to prove was that he ran the drugs smuggling for the IRA, but it came to nothing. We lost all contact with him and no concrete evidence could we manage to associate with him. I had a strong suspicion that McCreary and a few others ended up in Colombia with a drug cartel. Gordon Burns, we now know was there.'

Isbel was looking at the other unknown person, pointing to him. 'Jim, looking at the way he walks, and his height and build. Would you not say he comes from Colombia?'

'I think you are spot on Isbel; he has that Maradona looks about him. So maybe somewhere in South America.'

Denny entered his den with Agent Freeman. 'What have you found Jim?'

Jim pointed to McCreary, and the Colombian, Agent Freeman took a closer look. 'Can we enlarge it, Jim?'

'Yeah, sure.'

After four runs, Agent Freeman was still not sure. 'Gordon Burns was seen with a suspect we believe is a Colombian, that wore an earring, it depicted a fruit bat hanging from his right ear. About an inch long, with little red rubies for eyes. And that's what I was looking for, the only pictures we have, are too grainy to get a direct recognition of him. The fruit bat earring is the only concrete thing we have on him.'

FBI Agent Keats had been busy on his iPad. 'Jess, we have another sighting, our contacts in Glasgow have picked up their location. They are setting up another team to keep surveillance on them in association with MI5.' The two American Agent huddled together looking at the iPad, checking the surveillance information that was being collected by their operatives.

Isbel looked over the Agent's shoulders to see what they were watching, her reaction to what she saw took them by surprise. 'The cheeky bastards that my apartment.' Isbel pulled out her phone and started to e-mail the Estate agents, to cancel her agreement with them.

Agent Freeman, seeing what Isbel was doing snatched the phone from her. 'Isbel, we need to keep them from knowing that we are watching them. You will alert them, that they are under surveillance. We will reimburse you, so that you are not out of pocket. But please don't rock the boat?'

Denny took Isbel to one side. 'Nothing has changed, allow us to find out what this is all about, we can't bring Allister back. We can find the truth of what has happened, then we can bring them all to justice. Work with us, not against us?'

Isbel looked straight at him but said nothing. The anger on her face showed how she felt. Her fist was clenched tight, revealing the white of the knuckles. Denny knew she wanted revenge, all the information he had obtained about her told him so, she will have her revenge, one way or another. It was for how long he could contain her. Isbel turned and headed to her room. The heavy steps Isbel took, was how she felt, trampling on those she wanted to hurt. This was not someone kicking dust, but grinding her heel onto someone's bones.

Agent Keats, watching her leave had seen raw recruits act in the same way when training had not gone right, wanting, so badly to take it out on something or someone. 'I get the feeling when that over coiled spring snaps, it will end up soaked in blood.'

Agent Freeman looked concerned. 'Could she jeopardise this operation?'

Denny thought it was time to give Isbel's story some airing, the two agents, Lottie and Jim sat listening to Denny as he related how Isbel's life had made her the person she is. 'Isbel had never been given any formal training, what she does is not from any manual. Isbel just knows what is required to protect herself. Todd Baker told me when he first started training with her to assess her ability for stunt work, she did not know how to throw a punch, so that it looked like it was connecting, that was not supposed to. She hit him full on. Todd said he had been hit by bigger men, but not as hard as Isbel. It was the way she delivers her punches; Isbel gets every ounce of weight behind them. Uses her body like a cobra, the speed with weight distribution, giving maximum impact. Though that is not the only thing there is to it, as to where she aims her punches with the combination of them. Erica, Todd's wife a fully trained CIA operative seemed like a pussycat to how Isbel can handle herself.'

Agent Freeman nodded. 'Yes, I understand what Todd is implying when you fight someone who has been trained to fight you have a chance to second guess what was coming, but a person who has that ability to fight like Isbel, you have no way to predict what's coming next.' Agent Freeman knew Erica when she was a CIA field officer, had partnered her, on a few operations. Knew her capabilities very well, he could judge Isbel on that basis.

Isbel stood by the window in the bedroom looking out, her brain was working on her plan. Her phone call to Hugh was not answered, so she left a text message. 'How is the weather your end?' Sitting on the bed, Isbel closed her eyes. Todd had taught her how to plan her moves through, it was all about timing with application. Isbel had gone through all the information that had come through from Glasgow, via Denny and Jim, she would leave Edinburgh alone, it was not her stamping ground. Isbel made it clear to herself that she must not interfere with that side of the investigation, it did not mean she could not stir the pot in Glasgow. The ping from her phone told it was a text message. 'Weathers fine' Isbel phoned Hugh; he answered straight away. 'Isbel there's a round-about at Livingstone on the A71, called Oakbank Park. Meet me Ten am tomorrow with Five hundred.'

Chapter 7.

Forage into Glasgow.

Breakfast was quiet, Lottie did most of the talking. Jim and Denny were planning their day, Isbel just listened. She knew that any tit-bit of information could be valuable. When breakfast was over Isbel helped Lottie to clear away. Then washed up, she needed to keep people thinking, that all was normal. The drive to Craighall industrial estate, she maintained a calm approach, again not to bring attention to herself. Explaining to Pete about meeting Hugh, Pete spoke to one of the mums, on how she could help Isbel, with the agreed benefit of fifty-pounds compensation for her services.

Hugh was waiting for them at the Oakbank Park round-about, the silver-grey van was on the back of a pickup truck. Shaking hands with Hugh, Isbel eyes were already inspecting the Van. It was a small LDV Cub, big enough for her needs, it was clean with no logos, or of any signwriting, so nothing conspicuous that it would stand out in a crowd. Isbel paid the mum and sent her back to Pete's Gym with the Micra.

Hugh explained the details of the LDV Cub. 'Isbel, I was commissioned to purchase eight commercial vans for a delivery company, this little van came in as part of a job lot. It was too small for their needs, which ment it did not meet their specification, so it's yours. I have sent the details to the DVLA, this is who it is registered under and insured with, it is under a year old, so it did not need an MOT certificate, so I could Tax it for the next six months. It cannot be traced to you, so if you dress and act as though you are a delivery driver, you should not bring attention to yourself. Isbel I'm doing this for Allister, the five hundred is to cover some of the expenses.'

Isbel thanked Hugh, then headed back to the Gym in the LDV Cub. She stored the van in one of the disused buildings on the industrial estate. Then went to have coffee with Pete, Mags and the mums. The first stage of the plan was now in place. Now Isbel needed to select her first victim, someone that was not on the radar, yet close to someone that was. though still not an innocent person.

Lunchtime at Denny and Lottie's, Isbel made sure she joined in with the general chit-chat. Making sure the questions she asked, did not seem suspicious. After lunch Isbel said she was going to read a book, that she had planned to read for some time, then went to her room. Isbel did not attempt to read, slept instead.

At dinner time Jim came and told her dinner was ready, once more Isbel keeping up appearances that things were normal, even to sit with Denny after dinner looking at what was happening on their surveillance monitor, storing any useful information in her head as possible. Making out having seen enough indicated she would go and read her book in bed. Once in the room, started sorting out the clothes she had bought from Matalan. Arranging the bed as though it looked as if it was being slept in, then slipped out though the window. Leaving the Micra at the house, she jogged to where the Van was stored. Then headed off into the night. Her destination was two properties in Coatbridge, that sat about two and a half miles east from the centre of Glasgow, these were on her list of longtime unused vacant lockup garages. Isbel needed to check the locks and how secluded they were.

The first property was far to open and not in a suitable location, then proceeded to the next property. This setup was better, it was situated at the rear of houses, next to a rail track. The padlock that secured the building was a standard pattern security type that could not be undone with bolt croppers. Isbel pulled on some latex gloves, then taking a little fob key holder wallet from her pocket, when opened there were no keys, but a set of lock picks courtesy from earlier days. She had confiscated them from Allister to stop him from getting into trouble, with the sort of friends that Allister had been running around with at that time. Isbel could not dispose of them, as Allister had stuck a photo of their parents onto the leather holder. It portrayed them when they were good parents, not the monsters they turned into. The feelers and picks came in various shapes and sizes and with a delicate touch, Isbel had soon unlocked the padlock. The lock-up garage showed signs that it was being used as a store. Carefully looking around at the boxes she noticed some were open, taking a good look at them she could see the contents were of a white powder, and not of a legal substance, in the way they were packaged. Some loose powder was visable touching it with her finger tasted it, she knew straight away what it was. Taking photos with her phone she would use this evidence if the need presented itself. At this moment, she needed to be discreet. Checking the hood was coving her head, she exited the lockup garage, making sure she left it as she found it. The drive back to Musselburgh keeping her speed moderate, so as not to bring attention to herself, reflected on what she had seen in the garage. Entering her room how she had left it through the window, then she noticed the teacup by the side of the bed. Its contents were cold, Isbel drank it just the same. This gave her the time frame to work with, noting how long it would take to get to Glasgow and back, allowing some in between time to achieve a chore.

***

Breakfast was about the activity that had happened during the evening. Interpol and the CIA had joined together with MI5 in the intelligence gathering, they were piecing all the information together, were now understanding what was being organised, although it still needed some clarity. Jim had now made all the CCTV cameras in the city operational and could now trace all the known villains that were on their list of suspects. Many of the vehicles these gangs were using had been identified and had tracers attached to them. Denny was keen to stress that they needed to locate how these villains were entering Britain undetected, and that was why Jim was there.

When Denny and Jim left the table, leaving Lottie and Isbel alone.

Lottie touched Isbel's hand. 'I placed a cup of tea by your bed last night, you were sound asleep, so did not wake you.'

'Yes, it was still warm when I woke to go to the bathroom.'

'So, when did you return?' Lottie's head had turned towards Isbel 'My hearing told me you were not there, there was no sound of breathing, then the draught from the window led me to believe that was how you left the house. But don't worry I did not tell anyone; you must have had your reasons.'

Isbel did not duck the issue, 'Yes Lottie, I needed to find out what time it would take to get in and out of Glasgow, then I might be able understand what is happening just to clear my head from all these accusations that are being aimed at myself. Lottie, I'm not a person to just sit on my hands forever. Knowing what everyone else is doing, I must not jeopardise their objectives, yet must act within the law. But I know Glasgow and the people, it's no different from any other City, with most of its inhabitants being decent law-abiding citizens. But there are those that will only look out for themselves, getting others to do their dirty work for them.' Isbel's look of anger as she thought about what she was about to say. 'The Burkes and Burns will always be with us, never satisfied with what they have, always wanting more.'

Lottie placed her hand close to Isbel. 'Denny is trying to do what is right, he knows full well how you feel Isbel. He has spoken many times of how you been portrayed in the wrong way, he wants to put that right, so be careful.'

'Yes Lottie, I have taken precautions to be careful.'

Lottie, reached over and held Isbel's hand. 'Did you find out anything last night?'

'Yes Lottie, a lockup garage which seems to be used as a store, the contents were of various drugs. So, I have noted it, yet have done nothing just left it as I found it. This could help us later to flush out those that are behind this drug smuggling operation. Lottie my brother died under interrogation; why I don't know, who by? That's what I need to know. What will I do? That will be determined by how I feel, at that precise moment of time, it will also depend on the circumstances that I might find myself in.' Isbel squeezed Lottie's hand. 'I've come a long way since my parent's degenerated lifestyle killed them; I have made mistakes, have learnt from them. I'm bound to make more mistakes, but as long as I keep a cool head, I should stay out of trouble.'

Lottie's smile was soft and warm. 'Do keep yourself save Isbel; I love your company. Denny and I will miss you, when you eventually leave us.'

Isbel placed her arm around Lottie and gave her a warm tender squeeze. 'I would not put you or Denny in any danger. I have acquired a small van to slip in and out of Glasgow unnoticed. I will also need hideouts, if I find myself in difficulties.'

Lottie lifted her free hand and placed it on Isbel hand. 'I know you won't put us in danger Isbel, but please don't put yourself in danger.' Her voice was sincere, Lottie meant every word and Isbel could feel its meaning.

Isbel nodded, she won't put them in any danger, that's why she had acquired the van if Isbel was noticed they could trace the McKay's Micra back to them.

At the Craighall gym, Pete, Mags and the mums were already there when Isbel arrived. The lively atmosphere they generated warmed Isbel, as Isbel threw herself into her training regime; Mags and three of the mums tried to keep up with her, but they soon gave up. Most of the Mums just liked to watch Isbel, Mags explaining the benefits of each sequence that Isbel performed. Later as Isbel drank coffee with them, the Mums started asking questions from Isbel on why she did so much training. When Isbel explained the stunts and the TV and films she had worked on and the different fetes she had personally performed, they soon realised how important the training meant to her. 'Come, help me to clear these mats away I will show how to do the Kalotsky kick dance. The one that the Russian Soldiers perform, it helps with balance and gives you strength in the whole of your legs.' When the mats were cleared, Isbel crouched down and was soon into the kicking dance, as the mums clapped the rhythm. The few mums that tried to emulate Isbel, found it harder, then when at first it seemed easy.

Pete stood back watching the fun the mums were having, could see how Isbel's effect on them was showing good results. As the mums were enjoying the workouts, they were becoming fitter without feeling it was hard work. The mums knew that Isbel needed secrecy. Pete and Mags had allowed the mums a cheap rate, they realised it was beginning to pay them a good return. All Pete and Mags will have to do is find a way to keep it going when Isbel eventually goes. Looking at how it was going at this moment Pete did not seem too concerned about how it would turn out in the end. He had put much thought to how it could implicate them all, had sat with the mums and explained what could happen to Isbel. If it did not go to well for her.

Isbel said goodbye to them all, she needed to get some sleep before she ventured out towards her next evening excursion into Glasgow, yet she needed to find out if Denny and Jim had learnt anymore on what was happening.

Lottie was pleased to see Isbel when she arrived home, as Denny and Jim were now so concentrated on what was happening, were not communicating with her. She was feeling somewhat isolated, knowing when Isbel came back from the gym, she would have something to say. With the blindness, Lottie's other senses came into more effect; her sense of smell and her hearing could pinpoint where the sounds came from. The front door latch clicked, as Isbel's firm touch levered down on the door handle, then as the door opened, the rush of air that followed. Lottie picked up the soft smell of Givenchy Isbel often wore very sparingly, just a dab here and there enough to make her smell fresh but not enough to attract attention to herself. Lottie waited knowing Isbel would soon seek her out. Sure enough, the footsteps and the slight movement of air coming towards her would be Isbel.

Isbel touched Lottie's hand and with a soft, caring voice. 'Hi, you okay?'

'Yes Isbel, lovely seeing you (To Lottie hearing and smelling was like seeing) how did it go?'

'Good.'

'So what have you planned for tonight?'

'Another reccy, so I know where I can make my escape routes if needed.'

'Do you think you may need them?'

'That's the sixty dollar question I always ask myself, Lottie, with so many people involved I must take precautions to protect not only myself but those that are near to me. Denny is giving me good advice, to allow the Law to do its bit, that means I should respect him by taking his advise onboard. But the authorities have to play to the letter of the Law, the villains don't. It gives the villains advantage over the law. Yes, I want my revenge, but I also want these villains caught.'

Lottie understood why Denny had faith in Isbel. She may be a loose cannon, but she was an honest loose cannon. He could trust her, in many ways. Like how she handled Kenny, anyone with that amount of pent up anger would have beaten Kenny to a pulp. But Isbel wanted to find the truth first. Lottie thoughts, also knew that way behold, the guilty person when she does finally finds the truth.

'So. no heroics?'

'No Lottie, I don't know enough to take action at this time, so I must prepare myself for when I do know.'

Isbel bent down and kissed Lottie on top of her head. Lottie liking this reached up and placed her hand on the side of Isbel face. 'Take care Isbel, don't take too many risks. You have your whole life in front of you.'

'So did Allister, but someone took it away from him. They may believe they have had some fun, but wait till I play with them. The smile on their faces will not be of laughter, but that off the grimace of pain.'

Lottie felt the tension, as Isbel's body tightened up. The hand Isbel had on Lottie's shoulder became firmer, where before it had only rested there. Isbel stood up. Lottie could hear Isbel breathe deeply through her nose, then expel through her mouth, taking as much Oxygen into her lungs as possible, and exhaling the carbon dioxide out from her lungs. The calming effect was almost immediate.

'Sorry Lottie, I still need to find out why, and there is one person that does know. When I can find a way to travel without anybody knowing, I will seek her out. Lottie. the frightened look on Jacklyn's face showed she knew what had happened. Jacklyn Kennedy is the key, to open this sordid box of garbage.'

Lottie stood up. 'Come Isbel, let's get Denny and Jim to find a way for you to locate her. Get you away from here that will give the various authorities a chance to sort out what is what, without you interfering with their investigations.'

They both entered the room where Denny and Jim were working, they had installed many monitors, that were all working at the same time, in various location that were being watched simultaneously. Denny was concentrating on Edinburgh, Jim on Glasgow. Lottie touched Denny, and he removed the speaker headset he was wearing. The look he gave Lottie was a caring look.

'What can I do for you sweetheart?'

'How can we get Isbel away from here, so she can find Jacklyn Kennedy?'

It was Jim that answered. 'I can sort that out, Interpol have been searching for her as soon as we informed them of Jacklyn.' And he instantly started punching out text into the computer. The reply did not take long coming up on the screen. Denny looking at what the text said.

'I know where that is.' Turning to Isbel. 'You have two hours to pack a bag, I will in the meantime, find out where it is you are going.'

Isbel soon had her bag packed, making sure her passport was secure inside it. Denny and Jim had gathered the information that Isbel needed, Jim had it all printed and placed in a folder for her. Denny went to sort out the Micra, while Jim explained what they had done.

'A helicopter with Interpol's agent, Clive Philips, will pick you up. Then you will be taken to Paris to assist them. As Jacklyn Kennedy knows you, when you eventually meet up, this will help her to trust them.' Jim gave Isbel a folder that contains all the information they have gathered so far. 'Good luck Isbel, see you when you return.'

Lottie approached Isbel and opened her arms. The hug lasted for a few moments when Lottie released her grip holding Isbel hands. 'Take care, this could be the way forward to finding the answers you need Isbel, let's hope you are successful.' Lottie gave Isbel another hug, then kissed her cheek with the warmth of a mothers love. 'Haste ye back, Isbel.'

Denny appeared, for the hurry up. The drive to the rendezvous did not take long, the field where the helicopter was to land, was on the far end of the Racecourse. Then the light beaming down was from the helicopter, Denny flashed his lights. The Helicopter could now set down and land.

Isbel reached over and kissed Denny on his cheek, that was all that was needed.

Denny nodded his approval, reached cross and squeezed her arm.

Isbel grabbed her bag and headed towards the waiting helicopter. And as soon she was inside of the helicopter, the door was slid closed, it was up and away.

Isbel noted that the Pilot hugged the coastline, then near to Newcastle it headed inland. The airfield was Newcastle International where a private Jet was waiting and as soon as the helicopter touched down a young man raced over to take Isbel's bag. And ushered her towards the little Cessna Citation Mustang. Isbel climbed the few steps up to the entrance where the lean, five foot eleven; well dressed, clean-shaven all over the head, of West Indian parentage, introduced himself. 'Agent Clive Philips.' And directed Isbel to take a seat. The seats faced each other with a small table between them. Isbel sat and placed the folder on the table and buckled herself up, as the plane gathered speed, as it taxied down the airstrip. It was soon airborne.

Isbel's job took her to many places, so was use to air travel, soon as she was settled, gave the folder to agent Clive Philips. 'Denny McKay and Jim Anderson, have compiled all the information on what they know already, it's all here in this folder.'

Clive pulled the folder towards himself and started to turn the pages. 'Wow…this is so detailed.' And carried on reading, while Isbel sat back in the luxurious cream coloured leather seat. She felt the plane bank and took a new course, they were avoiding air traffic over airports. A monitor attached above their heads showed the course they were taking; Paris. Isbel felt calm.

The lad that had shown her too the plane, now placed a carafe of water with a slice of lemon, with some glasses on the table. Then poured some of the water into two of the glasses.

Clive sipped his water while reading, then looking up at Isbel. 'We are heading for Paris to meet the team that has been trying to find Jacklyn Kennedy. Denny has given us much help with this, he has confirmed you know Jacklyn Kennedy personally. This will be an advantage when we make contact. A known face may help to calm Jacklyn Kennedy, then we can extract the information we require, much more quickly.' Clive settled back in his seat, with a calm, relaxed manner. 'We have been monitoring some of these characters for sometime that have been found in Edinburgh, then they would vanish off the screen. To find them all together in one place, now that's a big worry. We are indebted to you for bringing Denny into this, if you had gone on your own, it might have just fizzled out, we would have been none the wiser to what was developing. The team are most interested in how you have responded, our reports on you give out mixed messages. Though we can trust Denny McKay, on our past involvements with him. Denny has said you believe that Jacklyn knows the answers to your brother Allister's death. Interpol shares those same feelings.'

The Pilot giving them the information that they were about to land, interrupted their conversation, but Agent Clive Philips had noticed how Isbel listened, taking everything onboard, not interrupting. Denny was right, give her respect she will respond likewise and give you her trust. The plane landed at Aerodrome de Chelles, near to east of Paris. The weather was good as Isbel stepped down the few steps onto the landing strip. Agent Philips directed Isbel too a waiting vehicle, the lad on the aircraft loaded her bag into the boot of the car, when they were seated, it sped off not heading into Paris but kept to the outskirts. Isbel had kept an eye on the directions; the journey took just under threequarters of an hour, they were now south-east of Paris. There was no sign attached to the electronically controlled gates to say why the house was there, the long drive up to the massive house showed it was to keep its secrets.

An elderly man with grey hair and a neat moustache stood there with a thirty-year-old woman. The car came to a stop close to them. Clive was first out and beckoned Isbel to follow. Where Clive introduced the pair to Isbel. 'Major Rupert Dupree and Agent Annette Monet.'

Isbel shook their hand. 'Please to meet you.'

They beckoned Isbel to follow them, the driver with Isbel's bag followed behind. Major Dupree spoke excellent English with a hint of a French acsent. 'You will stay here with the team to see how we work; gathering the information to the whereabouts of Miss Kennedy. Agent Monet will be your partner, you will share a room together, so that you get to know each other, to how we work together as a team. This is important, in such a serious situation as we believe what is happening in Scotland, which could affect the whole of Europe.' With a slight pause. 'This could have very dire complications to us all.' They stopped at the stairs. 'Annette will show you where you will be staying, freshen up and we will see you for dinner, where you will meet the rest of the team.'

Annette opened the door, into a medium sized room. The clinical look of the all white walls, and sparse furniture. Was for practical living, not permanent accommodation, the compact close fibre carpet tiles, also set the tone of easy clean, no-nonsense living quarters, down to the roller blinds at the windows, plain and simple. The beds were of similar design, iron-framed somewhat like the first NHS hospital beds use to look like. Sitting down on the mattress it felt firm with a little give. Isbel slowly surveyed the surroundings.

Annette showed her the bathroom, again practical with no frills. 'The shower it is a bit hit and miss, it may be hot just a fraction of a turn, it will be cold. I jump in and out again, just to freshen up.'

'Well, there is only one way of finding out.' Isbel headed back to her bed placed her bag on it, then unzipped it. Retrieved her toiletry bag, then started to remove her clothes folding them as she took them off.

Annette pulled opened some drawers in a nearby cabinet. 'Here you can use these towels' Annette then went and sat on her bed, watching Isbel strip down. Taking a close look at the long legs, and well-trimmed body. The muscles were firm, especially her sixpack tummy muscles. Isbel's butt was like her breast well rounded with no sag. Annette first thoughts. 'If I was gay, this is the type of girl I would like to have sex with' Annette's thoughts dwelled on that vision, then sighed. 'Then I'm not.' She watched Isbel head for the shower, Annette, had not stopped thinking how Isbel looked, for in a way the look was masculine, and thinking of some of the men she had dated, that were more feminine, then realised why she felt the way she did. Still watching Isbel, Annette was surprised when Isbel turned the shower to cold and stepped in, did not jump straight back out again. Just carried on washing down her body.

When Isbel returned to the bedroom, still drying herself, Annette asked. 'Have you a boyfriend Isbel?'

'No, Annette I haven't, and you?'

'No Isbel, its the work, it not the best for relationships. I have had friends who were boys, but not the right boys.'

'Yes, I know what you mean, too young, too old yet all of the same age.'

Annette's facial expression changed, with her eyes looking towards the ceiling, having that 'Oh yes look,' thinking about her last relationship. 'And those that are so demanding.. yuck, they are the worst type.'

Annette admired the lingerie that Isbel was changing into. 'That is not what I expect Isbel, I read the report on you. It came over as butch, Tomboy, yet you have nice taste.'

'It's because working on film sets Annette, you pick up all kinds of good advice. Lizzy, the wardrobe mistress, gave me many tips on how to dress to impress. And most of all, what kind of fabric is good or bad. The makeup girls, on how to get the best tones, and how to look after my hair. Listen and learn that all you need to know.'

'Well, they did a good job.'

Then Isbel showed Annette her makeup bag, it was simple. Yet held what was right for her, the colour tones suited Isbel complexion. 'This is all that I need, that's all there is to know, I have no need for anything else. I have no intentions to attract advances from the opposite sex, so, it's just for personal reasons to look and feel good.' When Isbel had finished dressing and sitting on the bed, her thoughts were about herself, and of her own needs. 'Annette my life has had its problems, Though for a while,

I have concentrated on getting myself a decent lifestyle away from the problems of my past life. Losing Allister it has dragged me back to the reality that I must not forget, to what has been already orchestrated. I must accept, to be where I am, to make what I can, from the little I have to work with.'

As the girls walked to dinner, they both asked questions to find out about each other. Annette had done her homework on Isbel, Though this did not bother Isbel for she took things as she found them and acted instinctively. Returning answers, then turning them into questions, in a direct way to Annette, gave Isbel an idea how Annette looked at tight situations, hoping she could judge how Annette would respond under pressure. Would she freeze, or just run for cover, protect her partner, or herself. Isbel had taken on board all the advice from Todd and Erica when they were just killing time, between their work schedules, Isbel had listened to their stories of the different situation they had found themselves in, with the reasons why they had acted to those conditions. Then Isbel would set up her training, to see how she could respond if she found herself in their shoes, practising over and over again to drill it permanently into her head. These situations would help when doing fight scenes, to make them look authentic.

There were eight for dinner, where Major Dupree introduced them. Agent Philips and his partner Luc Suttner, a Forty-year-old Swiss from Bern, thick set with a warm smile. With Annette these were the field team, the others were the Computer Support team, headed by Javi a fair haired, twenty-eight-year-old Fin from Nivala. Again It was Isbel listening and learning. The team had managed to piece together as much information about Jacklyn

Kennedy as they could, as soon as the team knew who they were supposed to find. They followed the paper trail of Jacklyn Kennedy. They knew she was scared and had just kept moving, and was not pursuing any set pattern for travelling. Which they had found, she had a good reason not too, for the team had discovered evidence that others were on her trail. The last sighting was in Avalon, now it was the wait for any clues where Jacklyn might be.

Javi a cool laybacked Fin, who was very relaxed. 'I've used all the information and set up a possibility program, this is to say if she would travel to any country within a two thousand mile radius, by using what knowledge we have learnt from how she has behaved, on the basis where JK had been and done before, that has given us possibilities. We have placed people to keep surveillance in various location. We have positioned ourselves here, just so we could reach those places by helicopter, in about two to three hours.'

Major Dupree, responded to Javi. 'The problems that we have been faced with are that we notified all police stations to keep an eye out for her, to pass any information they had on anyone with Jacklyn's description. The Major also had asked them to make sure she is protected at all cost. Though we are beging to believe, that some policemen have passed information to those that seek her. The worry is, have they found her first? It has been a week since the last sighting of Jacklyn.'

After dinner, Javi showed Isbel his computer room and how the program, he had set up actually worked. The map on the largest of the monitor screens showed the places that JK had been to, then where the possibilities of places that could be, they were coloured coded to say what was hot, and what was cold. Red was hot, Blue being cold, then a blue spot turned green. Javi surprised Isbel how quick he was to react, the computer showed a sighting in Adria, in the province of Rovigo. Italy. The rest of the team was soon there, eyes glued to the monitors; and like Denny, they were hitting all the CCTV cameras they could. Not a word was spoken for about an hour, till it was declared a false alarm. The local police had intercepted the suspect and confirmed she was clear. This was better for Isbel she felt, at last, she was involved.

After that false alarm, Isbel followed Annette to their bedroom when inside prepared themselves for bed. Annette laughed when she saw the white cotton onesy that Isbel wore for bed.

'I was bitten by bed bugs in a Morrocan Hotel, never again.'

Then looking at herself in the modest size of a mirror, that sat on the set of drawers, Isbel had to smile also. For she looked like a giant white Rabbit. But it was more like the coverall that the forensic teams use. The pair laid back in their beds still talking about themselves, the little personal thing that girls always seem to talk about. Then now again Annette would throw in a more direct question.

'Alex Burke's son Robert, you lost your cool and did some serious damage to him. The report showed you had blinded him in one eye and disfigured his face. The police report, said you attacked him over some remark he made?'

The look on Isbel's face when she heard Annette comment. 'Some remark he made?' Isbel could only laugh. 'Robert Burke, and his two shadows, Erskine and

Greer. They were eighteen, I was fifteen. Their comment was 'You act like a man, but we are going to turn you into a woman.' This was in the local park, I had gone there to fetch Allister for his tea. That's where I found Robert Burke bullying Allister; Yes Annette, I admit losing my cool. Three large louts setting on one fifteen-year-old lad, was not my idea of acting fair. I lashed out and hit Burke, catching him on the side of his head. Erskine grabbed me from behind, as Greer grabbed Allister. Then Burke punched me twice in the face, then Erskine dragged me back along one of those single plank benches. With Burke grabbing my legs, spreading them and standing between them with his knees bent kneeling onto my legs, I found I could not move as Robert Burke used his penknife to cut my knickers. Then undid the top of his trousers, pulling me towards him, he penetrated me, Erskine seeing Burke performing, relaxed his grip. That was enough for me to breakfree and grab the buckle of the belt that Burke had used to hold his trousers up, with the strap in my hand and the buckle resting on and between my thumb and forefinger, the buckle tongue entered his eye as I swung at his head, then dragging the buckle tongue down his fce. The scream Burke gave out, as he rolled off me, dragging me off the bench, that alerted the park warden. As the Parky rushed forward to where we were, he saw me putting the heel of my shoe into Burke's face. I had also managed to kick out at Erskine breaking three off his ribs. then jumping on the back of Greer, who was still trying to contain Allister; pushing my fingers up into his nostrils, then yanking upwards, this act dislodging his nasal bone that need surgery to put it right. That was giving them as much pain as I could. When Allister recovered from what had happened, managed to pull me away from Greer. Did the police put that into the report?... No, they twisted the whole story around to protect Burke's son. Then there was the lack of the doctor's report, that got misplaced giving the evidence of penetration. And the forensic evidence of my knickers that were cut with Roberts penknife. The lack of this evidence presented the jury with no choice but to conclude without that vital evidence, it was more of a case of assault then rape. An inquiry was set up to find out, how the essential evidence was mislaid. Yet, no answers given to why there was no trace of any reports found in the system. Though the Police Doctor and the Forensic team said they had carried out the test. Burke and Burns were cleared of any wrongdoings.'

Annette had listened carefully. 'So, you don't trust the police?'

'Annette, Major Dupree commented on how some policemen had given the other side information about Jacklyn Kennedy, does that mean he doesn't trust all the police forces that he as to work with?'

Annette nodded, she accepted Isbel's reply. Then wanted to know if the rape had produced an un-wanted outcome.

'No Annette, the Police Doctor gave me an EC. You know the Morning after pill? For my peace of mind. Even the record of that, was not found. All though I still had to sign the form, that I had received and taken it in precence of the Doctor.' Isbel shook her head remembering the way the Police Doctor had purposely gone through explaining the function of the EC pill to her. 'Annette, where I come from, you have to act tough, or you suffer. There is always somebody that wants to take advantage of someone's else's weaknesses. Allister was no saint; then again, nor was I. We did what we had too, that was to survive. That's all there was to it. My father could not take the indignity of losing his job and crept into the bottle, then when that did not give him the blanket to hide under, started smoking pot. Drink and pot are not good bedfellows, but when mum sunk down to his level. That's what made life so hard for Allister and myself. Dad would lash out with his fist, at anyone that disagreed with him. So, I learnt to fight back, until he realised he could not live up to his manhood. I had not won the battle, I just gained a little ground. It became my life to take control of what was around me, that's now in my genetic makeup. But Todd and Erica were slowly turning my life around, getting me to understand myself. That was to take control, to be able to take a deep breath and think through my actions. This I found to be what I needed, keeping calm and calculated. Then acting with speed and commitment.'

Isbel paused for a moment, contemplating what Erica had implied to her about how she looked in other peoples eyes. 'One of the sketch artist on the set, drew two images of myself, the first showed me how I really looked, an elegant young lady. The second image showed me as the person that I represented, in how I spoke; drink-sodden, cigarette hanging down from my mouth. Tattoo's covering my body, sloven attitude, in all a slob. It was a smack in the face with a cold, wet haddock, but I got the message. I had to get myself, some form of control.'

Isbel pondered on those days, working out on how she wanted to be. Todd had already mentioned before about the communication problem they had with her. This made it clear she needed to conform or lose everything.

'Annette, I observed all of the people around me. I started to see what I could do to make the changes. Made friends with people that I could see would be how I could end up portraying; not too posh, of air and graces, but with clear and precise vocabulary, it worked. They helped with the transformation, correcting me when I slackened, and fell back to my old slang ways. Slowly it did work, Erica was there overseeing the transformation, offering advice where it could help.'

Chapter 8.

The Hunt for JK.

The morning felt different to Isbel, she was awake before Annette. Using a chair, Isbel was doing ballet routines, these stretching exersizes, were mainly for flexibility, but more important self-control and balance.

Annette woke to see Isbel going through her paces doing vertical splits, with both of her legs looking like an extended pole holding the ceiling up, with Isbels hands extended up to her ankle, of her upstretched leg. Annette laid there watching, just as the mums at Pete's gym found her fascinating, so did Annette, who did not want Isbel to stop. Seeing Isbel completely naked going through with such grace and with such discipline, remembering her own feeble attempts when she had gone to ballet classes as a young girl.

'Where did you learn to do that Isbel?'

'Erica wanted me to do a special stunt, paid for ballet school training for four weeks. It paid off, as I carried the stunt out. The Director was most pleased. He paid for myself to do another four weeks of training, for a special film he was doing about a Prima ballerina. The bonus brought me my Audi A3.'

Isbel gently wound down her exercises, then showered. Walking down to breakfast Isbel wanted to know how much she could get involved with finding Jake. Annette was all smiles.

'That's why you are here, is it not? To get involved and assist us?'

Isbel nodded, she knew that finding Jake was the key to open up this can of worms.

With breakfast over, it was time to catch up what had been happening during the night. The program had not changed, the colour mapping was still where it was when Isbel was there the night before. Isbel took over a spare computer, Annette helped to bring the case file up. Isbel started to check on the places they had known where Jacklyn had been sighted. Isbel began from where JK had landed when she fled from Glasgow. Malaga, then JK disappeared the first known town was in the north of Spain a small village called Villablino, working for anyone who wanted her. Then a strange car was seen, JK vanished. The next known was another small town, Paramo Del Sil. when once more had suddenly disappeared. A family from Velilla Del Rio Carrion, reported that a girl who had been working for them had left without her wages, was concerned that maybe something could have happened to her. Pamplona was the next stop. Then Saint Pe D'ardet in Andorra. Now Avalon. Isbel Googled these places. Mountains. Then it clicked.

'Javi, when Jacklyn arrived at Malaga, was there a police report on a stolen, mountain bike?'

It did not take them long to find out. 'Yes, there was an Orange Alpine 6e, electric powered mountain bike stolen the next day.'

The smile of knowing from Isbel. 'That's it JK is using the mountains to flee whenever danger looms, we need to look at small mountain Towns preferably in northern Italy.'

Annette Googled the Mountain bike. 'Wow, seven thousand Euro's for a bike.'

Isbel looked over Annette's shoulder. 'Yes Annette, but that one is electrically assisted. No need to buy petrol can travel anywhere. What more could JK need to be able to travel undetected? Lyca racing gear and a safety helmet? As cycling is so popular in Europe who would take a second look at her.'

Clive and Luc pulled up their chairs nearer to Isbel and Annette. Luc was the first to pick up on what type of a girl JK was.

Isbel did not need time to think, responded straight away.

'Like all kids born on these local council estates all around the world, they have to adapt. You use what you can, by choosing the right friends. You look after them they look after you. Just as all of you have to do, to do your job, you have to rely on each other. As any youngsters would tell you, mobility is their main objective: rollerskates, skateboards, but the king of all transport, the bike.'

Luc, nodded. 'That tells us how she is getting pass everyone, Though how does she think, what makes her tick?'

'Yes Luc, as I first said, she will adapt. She probably arrived at Malaga, with some money in her pocket knowing it had to last her; she would then head into town to mingle or get lost in the crowd. Then she would look to see what could she use to her advantage, the bike must have been seen for her to realise it's potential. I would expect her to purchase the right clothes to hide even though she could be seen. Stealing that bike, now that could have been more luck then just planning I would presume; so would want more detail on how it was acquired. The rest of the plan is to keep moving, a rolling stone gathers no moss. To loiter too long you will be recognised by many, but stay for short spells, by just a few.'

Major Dupree and the other members had gathered around. And now it was a debating group. The Major needed to encourage this type of examination of JK if she was to be able to help them to understand what these Criminal Organisations were up to.

Major Dupree had realised what Isbel was saying. 'That gives us to where we are now, but we need to know what she would be looking at, being able to survive now?'

Isbel acknowledged 'Yes Major, Taking the routes she has taken, I would say that the first sign of trouble or doubt, she would head for the hills. Any mountain foot track would do just to give her space, but not open space. Once she knows she is clear, then she would be able to rest. To take bearings, then make a judgement on where the next stop could be. Keeping to small towns, with many exits to hills or mountains.'

Annette more thinking as a girl would think. 'Would she not look to be a bit unkempt, and stand out to people, that she is a vagrant of some sort.'

'Not really Annette, JK's first family home was old and had no central heating. So JK was used to washing in cold water, then being particular how she looks. I know when the school went camping during the school holidays, she was always the first one to jump into the lakes no matter how cold the conditions were. JK never took a lot of clothes, would wash them and dry them in the bushes. As soon as they were dry would bash them on a rock to loosen the material, but she always looked clean.'

'So that why we are finding it hard to detect her.' Luc made a note, then he produced a picture of JK caught on a CCTV camera. 'This was captured while JK worked at a packing plant in Pamplona, that's the only reason we knew she had been there. The name she gave was Ann Scott. When the packing plant company got a notification that her identity was false, she had disappeared. When I interviewed the owner, that when we found out that there were others on her trail. We have some photo's of those that are trying to find her, but as yet, we can't identify them.'

Javi came into the group. 'I've put a search into the area that Isbel has pinpointed, this one looks more likely, as we have had a report that a sighting has been made near Bouge en Bresse near the Swiss boarder. It was caught on a CCTV camera in a Café, we should be getting the video at any moment.'

As they turned their attention to the monitor, Clive commented on how hard it would be for JK to cross into Switzerland. The border checkpoints would be more stringent than the EU border points. The monitor showed JK at a table studying a map. One of Javi's team was trying to see what the map was showing. Annette was more interested in JK herself, her hands, face, what she was wearing, even how JK drank her coffee, then when JK was about to leave the cafe she emptied the sugar sachets from the table into her pocket. 'Instant energy,' Annette commented.

Major Dupree, was satisfied with how it was turning out. 'Team we are going down the right track, where we have been trying to see where she had been, we now can make a plan to place where she might be.'

Then Javi put up on the screen an area that the program had selected. 'Grenoble'.

'But that's a large town,' Annette exclaimed.

'Yes it is, but on the eastern side of Grenoble it has many small suburbs around it, and they're at the base of mountains.' Javi persisted. 'We are monitoring the area right now, using all the CCTV cameras that cover the more likely routes JK would take. And as we have teams already in that area, we should be able to establish ourselves quite quickly.'

The Major took the decision to send the team there immediately. And instructed the Helicopter to prepare for take-off.

Annette indicated to Isbel, to make their way to their room to collect their things. When they were packing, Annette thanked Isbel.

Isbel did not understand. 'Why Annette?'

'We were going nowhere Isbel, sitting about waiting for something to happen. Since you arrived, the wheels are now moving in the right direction.'

The Helicopter was heading for the Airdrome Le Grenoble. LeVersoud. A small airstrip. Two rental Peugeot SUV vehicles were waiting for them, they were met by Agents Bernard Lennard and Toni Buchet. Annette was soon embracing Toni, they had joined Interpol together and had partnered each other on three different operations. After the introductions, the men were heading for St-Martin D'uriage, the girls were going to Belmont. Both houses sitting at the foot of the Alps. Both near the two routes that went over the Alpes, though not the main roads. This was the criteria set by Isbel. The house in Belmont was much the same as the other house in St-Martin's they were situated in Cul-de-Sac's that usually rented out to Skiers. Toni a thickset girl in her thirties, with a beautiful easy going personality. Isbel took to her instantly, as Toni was direct, saying only as she viewed what she saw. When Toni shook Isbel's hand for the first time. 'You are stronger than you look, you match your description on our records of you.' Isbel knew she was not trying to be polite, but honest.

Toni Buchet explained the setup. 'We have been here for a year, there has been a series of incidences that needed observation, relating to a bizarre case of identity theft, and blackmailing of three prominent government officials, that were heavily involved with the European Parliment. We were just about to wrap up here when Headquarters ask us to stay put. Johanna Clemont will be arriving later. You two don't mind sharing, Johanna is not the tidiest of girl you would meet, but she is the most trustworthy there is. Oh yes, she also snore very loudly, so better to have her own room?'

Johanna arrived an hour later with supplies, which they all helped to carry in. Then as they packed the supplies away, the introduction was slightly haphazard. Johanna's English took a lot of understanding, but in the end, it got better. Isbel's French also improved. The bubbly blonde Johanna, with her pudding face, did the cooking, That's when Isbel understood how tidy, she was not. Then to how the food tasted, that was so different, could see why Toni did not mind the mess. Over dinner, the talk was on Jacklyn Kennedy. Johanna hit on why the other people were finding out where JK was. 'These bikes are expensive, so the owners have a tracking device fitted. The signal it give out, is over a short distance only. That's why they have not caught her as yet... I have already enquired about the signal code, and have set it up. So I can add the app into your mobile phones.'

Isbel knew how it worked it was the same as Denny had installed on her phone to keep track of her at the hotels in Edinburgh. Johanna set the device, on their phones, while the girls cleared the third world war debris in the Kitchen. They all agreed it was well worth it. The two way talk between the two houses, had Bernard coming to them with their phones, to have the tracking device installed, also with any other updates that Johanna could give them. So not only was Johanna a good cook, but also good with computers. As Toni and Annette had much to catch up on. Isbel found herself sitting with Johanna, watching and learning. Out of the four monitors, Johanna had set up, one had four split images of the roads that were not covered by the CCTV traffic control cameras on the main roads into Grenoble. Johanna had previously set cameras to cover these routes for the previous surveillance they had been working on. The image of JK in the Café, was on another screen, which Johanna was scanning, the same as Denny had done to find Allister at Edinburgh Waverley. Johanna set the program running then turned to Isbel. 'We'll find JK, then she will be safe from harm.'

The smile warmed Isbel, she came here to seek the truth as well, the two went side by side.

Then Toni came into the room and touched Johanna's shoulder. 'Go get some sleep, it is nearly Twelve, Annette will relieve me at three, then you relieve her at seven.' There were no objections, and Johanna left the room.

Toni sat down in front of the monitors. 'This is the easy part, just sit and keep watch. Johanna has her faults, but she is so good at what she can do right.' Toni meant precisely what she said, and Isbel knew what she had said, was correct. For in her way, Johanna was as capable as Denny with computers.

When Isbel eventually went to bed the large king size bed that she was to share with Annette looked so inviting. Isbel did not put on the onesy, but slipped into bed naked, the Snow goose down duvet, felt so soft yet so warm and was soon fast asleep.

***

At Four, Toni woke her. 'Isbel wake up we have a sighting.'

Isbel shot out of bed grabbing clothes. She pulled on her jeans and a jumper, then followed Toni to where Annette and Johanna were studying the Monitors. Toni had a street map of the area and needed help to find the exact place that JK was heading for. Isbel had soon established the road JK was heading down, as Toni informed the men.

Bernard was quickly issuing orders and was looking for a suitable location to be able to intercept, and make contact with JK without scaring her. Annette was reading out the position that was showing on the monitor. The first sighting was on the Rue Albert Girard Blanc. At four fifteen, then entering Route De Grenoble. Then it showed JK had turned off into the Montee du Champ de la Vigue.

Bernard could see the bleep on his Phone. 'We have contact, Clive has his iPad set up. So we can track her, you better get Isbel here as soon as you can. We need her to make the contact.'

Toni agreed as Isbel finished dressing. The drive to St Martin D'uriage took fifteen minutes. Clive met them at the door and ushered them in. 'JK has stopped, we believe she is surveying the terrain, making plans for her next move. We will know which plan we must take when she moves.'

Bernard showed them the three possible contact points. 'These are the best places, where we can stop JK without harming her.'

Luc spoke up. 'She on the move. Plan B, she heading for Chapen.'

The team jumped into the cars, Bernard got behind the driving wheel of the vehicle that Toni and Isbel arrived in, as he drove, he went over the plan of action with them. They sped around the roads leading to Chapen, it was not for the faint-hearted with the twist and tight turns with the many hairpins because of the hilly terrain. The place the team had chosen was in a valley, the road JK was taking would take her down into the valley then a tight turn, to head up Route Vernon. 'With many trees either side, JK would ride into a bottleneck with no risk of any harm towards her. With the cars parked up, the men set up their positions, Isbel stood with Toni in the road, just up the hill from the tight turn at the valley. Clive began the countdown as JK got closer, raised an arm telling them JK was there.

Jacklyn freewheeled down the Chapen and was getting ready for the sharp turn, then to pedal up the Route Vernon Hill, the tall figure standing there made her break, as three shadows appeared from the trees, she had nowhere to go. Then Jacklyn heard a familiar voice.

'Jake its Isbel I'm here to make you safe, my love.'

Jacklyn let go of the bike and sank to her knees, Isbel could see her shoulders moving with the sobbing, that Jacklyn was now uncontrollably behaving with, on the realisation that the chase for her was now over. Isbel went to her and knelt down beside her, placed a loose arm around her. 'Come sweetheart let's get you fed and put you to bed, we can go over the problems when you are ready.'

Toni brought the car up, and Jacklyn laid down on the back seat while Isbel sat in the front with Toni. Clive picked up the bike, the next stage of the plan, was for Clive to ride the bike back to the house in St Martin D'uriage. So, those that were tracking JK would believe she was still active. Interpol wanted to know who was behind them, so their capture was essential. Major Dupree and Javi had instigated the whole plan.

The vehicle with Jacklyn, arrived at the house in Belmont. Annette and Johanna came out to meet them, their concerned looks, helped Jacklyn to relax. Isbel took Jacklyn's arm into hers and patted the back of her hand in a comforting manner. Jacklyn now felt weak from the effort of trying to flee, worrying who was chasing her.

Johanna had been busy in the kitchen, the smell of home cooked food, drifted into Jacklyn's nostrils. With the feel of being wanted, was now washing over her in a lovely way.

Toni did not push for information. 'Do you want a bath Jacklyn, or just have something to eat, then go straight to bed?'

'Sleep would be nice.' Jacklyn's deep voice just purred with the thought of sleep. After food Annette showed Jacklyn where she could sleep, promised to stay with her to make sure she was safe, indicating to the Remington R51 9mm pistol that was there to convince JK she was safe.

Isbel assured Toni That she would keep an eye on the surveillance monitor so Toni could catch up on her and Johanna's sleep.

When morning eventually arrived, Toni made Isbel sleep. Isbel woke when Johanna brought her coffee. 'Jacklyn is still sleeping Isbel, Annette said that she kept tossing and turning for the first two hours, then she settled and slept like a log.'

When Isbel crept in to check on her, Toni was there keeping watch. 'She's fine Isbel let her sleep. I've spoken with the Major, we are to hold her here until we know what is happening with the boys. Bernard said it is all quiet there at the moment, Johanna had already set up a camera in the house and two outside, and is keeping a close lookout for them. Two more agents have been flown in to assist them. And have set themselves up close to the house. Javi reckons to-night might be when they would make a show. Two cars have been seen in the neighbourhood, they had Marseille plates. The way they circled around, they looked like professionals.'

Jacklyn stirred, then turned over and carried on sleeping. When Isbel took over from Johanna. It was late in the afternoon when Jacklyn woke to see Isbel smiling at her, she eased herself to sit up, Isbel joined her. Jacklyn had been thinking of what had happened and wanted Isbel to know.

'It was all my fault Isbel, I should have taken off there and then, but panicked, I did not know what to do, so I went to Allister for help. He let me stay at your place. And Allister went to Edinburgh, to see a friend to arrange somewhere for me to hide. When I saw Robert Burke watching the flat, I managed to sneak away, through the rear exit of the flats without being noticed. I phoned three times to tell Allister about Robert Burke, but it was only an answer phone that answered. Then on the fourth time of trying, Tom Burns answered, that's when I knew that it had not gone right for Allister. I made my escape, by taking the first plane I could get on at short notice. Reading about Allister's murder in the newspaper. I had to keep running, if they had done that to Allister, they would do the same to me.'

Isbel gave her a cuddle. 'Major Dupree, of Interpol, will need to know what you have seen, you will be flown to Paris where there is a safe house for you to stay till this has been resolved. What I came here to do is to find out, what you saw for all this to have happened. I want revenge for how they tortured Allister. Though I want to make sure that only the one that are really responsible, are the one that I will vent my anger on. For now, let's make you comfortable so you can concentrate on what has happened.'

Annette and Johanna were keeping a close eye on development at St Martin's, the two suspect cars had positioned themselves. The occupants of the vehicle were now maintaining surveillance, binoculars could be seen trained on the house. The Major had already acted, and a flotilla of Police vehicles had closed off all exits the trap was sprung as the two teams engulfed the two suspect cars. No resistance was given, as they surrended their weapons without any fuss. The police searched the garden of the house and found the bike it had a flat tyre. Clive had done that to make it look as if JK had abandoned it, then had fled. That was why the police found no sign of the suspect that had stolen it. Bernard explained he had rented the house while he was on business, with his two colleagues. The stories held up, the police were happy. This was to make those that were chasing JK think she was still on the run.

Toni waited for new orders, and as everything quietened. The Major gave his instructions. Toni laid down her phone. 'Annette, Isbel collect your things together, you are taking Jacklyn to Paris.' Jacklyn's glance at Isbel showed the relief she was now feeling.

Isbel gave Jacklyn a hug. 'You are going to be fine, you will be able to sleep, not worrying who is looking for you.' But Isbel could see the grief in Jacklyn's eyes, she was carrying a heavy burden believing she had caused Allister's death. Isbel with Jacklyn still in her arms cradled her, placing kisses on her forehead. 'Jacklyn you were not to blame for Allister, you were as much of a victim as Allister was in all of this. Now we are going to turn the tables with the help of these lovely people, whatever information you can give them, that's how you are going to revenge Allister.'

Jacklyn was very quiet on the flight to Paris, held a firm grip on Isbel's arm, Annette held her other hand. This was still hard for Jacklyn to understand, for what had and still was happening to her.

The Major was waiting in the grounds of the large chateau near Paris, as the helicopter touched down. Annette was out first and aided Jacklyn down, As the Major stepped forward to greet them. He did not say much, just welcomed her, and to show her to the house. Isbel and Annette collected the bags and followed them into the house. The Major had it all under control with those that were going to look after Jacklyn, were there in attendance.

As JK was led away to get a nice bath, Jacklyn turned smiled at Isbel and mouthed 'Thank you' Isbel nodded and blew her a kiss.

Major Dupree now turned his attention to Annette and Isbel. 'Shall we?' As he directed them towards the table, when seated he proceeded. 'Well done girls, Annette your main duties are to be Jacklyn's minder until this whole case is resolved. Isbel I know you came here to find the answers to this problem, so you will be here till you are satisfied you know what we know. Then you will be flown back to Scotland with Clive and Luc, who are going to link up with the organisations that are already there. Javi is working with Denny McKay, and with GCHQ. Since you been here much information has been gathered together, and with that information, to what we retrieve from Jacklyn, we hope to know how to respond to the threat we are facing. We will give Jacklyn time to conduct herself, so tomorrow morning we will listen to what Jacklyn has to say. This is not an interrogation, but a debriefing, Jacklyn has done no wrong in our eyes. So she will remember more if given the right reasons and conditions to do so.'

'Thank you, Major, for being honest with me and trusting in me.'

Major Dupree nodding in appreciation. 'Isbel, I will be honest with you. When I read the reports on you, I was concerned about how you were going to respond to meeting Jacklyn. We did not know if you would seek vengeance for your Brother's Murder on Jacklyn. So, we monitored you to be sure. The feedback I received was your concern for Jacklyn as a friend, it is what you said to her that pleased us most of all.

Annette's look towards Isbel, was business like. 'My report will say how you stepped up and helped when it was required, knew when to stand back, so not to get in the way.'

The Major followed up on Annette's comments. 'The whole team admired how you listened to everyone, yet did not interfere with what was trying to be achieved by them.'

Later when Clive and Luc arrived back from Grenoble, over the evening meal. Jacklyn listened to the general banter of them all. Isbel noticed how Jacklyn was relaxing in their company, her shoulders were more relaxed, not hunched up with tension, as when she had found herself trying to flee, from the terror of being discovered Now how Jacklyn sat in the chair, she was her old self again. Jacklyn started to talk about herself, the team were warming to her deep soft husky voice, as if she was a soulful jazz singer, singing a love ballad.

Major Dupree, watched with interest in how this was all going; yes he wanted answers, but he wanted the right answers. This thing that was happening in Scotland could have extreme ramifications if allowed to continue, not just for Scotland. The whole of Europe and beyond. So he must make sure he gets all the right information he can. He had warned the team that this was so important that they were here for the duration of the case, no leave, no matter what circumstances that cropped up must not interfere with the process of this operation. He even had recruited a larger team, then that was required, just in case something did happen to a member of the team he had an instant back up.

Jacklyn was the last one down to breakfast, she knew what was required of herself, and made sure she was ready. Walking up to Isbel, she held out her arms for a cuddle and Isbel duly responded. 'I'm ready Isbel, this is revenge for Allister.' The look in her eyes was of determination to tell her story as she had seen it.

Isbel lifted the hair from Jacklyn's forehead and gave it a long lingering kiss. 'Only the truth is needed my love that's all. Say it as you saw it.'

When Jacklyn had gone to bed. She had thought about what had happened that day. All night the images that unfolded in her head during that sleep time was now so clear she could remember everything as if it had happened just there and then. Although this had been going on, she had still slept soundly and was up for the task.

Cameras were set around the room, to record all that was said by everyone, not just Jacklyn. If this was needed in a Court of Law, they had to show, how they obtained the evidence. GCHQ was listening in on the interview. Each person, identifying themselves to the camera. Major Dupree set the scene asking Jacklyn to recall all that had happened.

Jacklyn composed herself. 'My Grandfather use to work on the old puffer boats, with his brother. And my father worked on and off for Billy Boyd on his boats doing roughly the same thing. I would now and again go down and give a hand usually just to clean the insides of the cabins. That Thursday old Mr Boyd asks if I would like to earn some extra money and clean out the cabin on his boat. I agreed to do it after work that evening. His boat was moored up at the dock, near where I live at Drumchapel. I just had to ride my Vespa Scooter down Yorker, into Dock Street. Where Boydfriend, the name of Boyd's boat was moored up.

Jacklyn took a sip of water, before proceeding.

I had been working for about an hour when A Sloop pulled up alongside and docked. Looking out of the starboard porthole, I saw four men leave the Sloop then they drove off in a bright blue Suzuki 4x4 Jimny. At the time I did not think much about it, as this sort of thing happens all the time. As the light started to fade inside the

Cabin, I had just finished and was clearing up when I heard the sound of a vehicle pulling up, I carried on collecting by bits together, then made my way up on deck, locking the cabin as I went. I turned to leave when I saw these men loading a van up with many boxes, I recognised Robert Burke, Nick Diplock and at first, I thought it was Tom Burns, I realised this Burns was a little older and weather-beaten, where Tom Burns is pasty looking. There was a short, stocky foreign guy with an earring in one ear, something black hanging down from it. I heard Robert Burke shout out to get her, I ran to my scooter. Pushed it off its stand, holding the clutch in, turning the gear selector at the same time, I just kept running, pushing the scooter then letting go of the clutch as I jumped on the seat and took off and headed up Yorker, with them close on my heels. With the Suzuki someway behind giving chase. I was panicking as my scooter has a top speed of forty miles an hour on a good day, that day was not a good day. Then I saw this lorry trying to turn, it was backing up across the road. I managed to get around it, but the Suzuki had to stop. I turned down a side road, there was a high fence outside a house, I drove my scooter through the gate and hid behind the fence, turning the ignition off so I could not be heard. The Suzuki drove past twice, though it did not stop. I stayed where I was. Later phoned Allister, he told me to make my way to Clarion Road where the Golf Course is, where we first had sex together.

Allister met me with Isbel's Audi A3. Then Allister took me to their flat, and I stayed there while Allister tried to find somewhere for me to stay. He had a friend called Kenny, that could help us in Edinburgh, but didn't know the address, Allister phoned Kenny, but he did not answer. So he left a message and took the train to Edinburgh. I waited at the flat, then the next morning I heard the letterbox open, when a long thing was pushed through it. I managed to conceal myself then it was pulled back, I stayed still for an hour. Then I peered out of the window trying hard not to disturb the curtains, I could see Robert Burke outside with two of Nick Diplocks men. I waited until the early hours of the morning when I could not see anyone, that's when I left.

I walked as far away from the flat and headed for an old relative of my mums. Who I knew she would lecture me, yet still would help. Stan, my cousin, told me that a reward of a thousand pounds had been circulated for my whereabouts. I left three messages, on the forth time I recognised Tom Burns voice and immediately hung up. It was Stan that drove me to the Airport.'

'Let's take a rest there,' Major Dupree had watched Isbel, her black piercing eyes had just narrowed. She now had names, he could read her face, knowing this is was not going to stop here. Isbel was keeping her anger under control, for how long? That is what they were to find out.

Drinks were given out, and Javi wanted to confirm that the information had been received by GCHQ. Luc spoke to the Major, and Clive joined in with the discussion. The Major turned towards Isbel. 'I believe you have heard all you need to know Isbel, We will organise a flight for you, I suggest you pack and meet Clive and Luc at twelve.'

Isbel now was holding Jacklyn's hand. 'When this is all over we must give Allister, our time and love at his funeral together.'

Jacklyn's look, was sad. 'Take care Isbel, they are not nice people. I don't know the full details what they did to Allister, and I don't want to know. Isbel, I only want to remember Allister for the person he was, I don't want his image tainted by what they did to him.'

'When this is all over Jake. I promise you, you won't have to look over your shoulder worrying who is after you.'

The Major watching them, could not see the person that the police report on Isbel portrayed. She was so different. Annette, Toni and Johanna only had kind words about her. Yet behind those eyes, there was trouble for someone. For there was no warmth in them, just the cold look of bitter hate. But he understood why, reading the complete story of Isbel's troubled upbringing from Alex McCallum and Denny McKay. Thinking if he had been in her shoes would he not behaved the same way? He also knew that she could create many problems for those who were trying to resolve what was happening in Edinburgh. Yet she could determine what was happening in Glasgow. He was treading a dangerous path in letting Isbel return, though having strong gut feelings about Isbel's ability in how she looked after those she had trust in, could be what is needed to flush out Burke and Burns. Major Dupree had seen all the reports on those two, the reports showed two dedicated Officers. Yet he could sense a smell of rotting decay from both of them.

Clive and Luc sat with Isbel on the flight back to Scotland, She was giving them the information on those that Jacklyn had said was on that boat. 'If they could bring drugs into Scotland in that quantity, that must be how they were bringing people in the same way. Isbel we are hoping that the satellite cameras will see how that is happening. The joint partnership with MI5, CIA and ourselves should be able to sort this out.'

Chapter 9.

Knowing the names.

Lottie's smile was so warm. 'Come, give me a hug, I've so missed you. Denny has been so involved in this, I have felt like a widow.' The hug from Lottie was big, Isbel could feel how Lottie had missed her. 'Now tell me what happened, and what did you find out?'

Isbel explained to Lottie all that had happened. 'Jake had seen this electric mountain bike being displayed at a large super store, went and purchaced the lycra cycling gear. Then wearing the outfit just walked into the store, then wheeled it out under everybodies eyes. She travelled by night mainly trying to put distance between herself and those that were chasing her, unaware that the bike she had stolen was electronically tagged. That how Interpol used that to track her.'

Lottie's look, hearing the audacious way that Jacklyn stole the bike. 'And nobody tried to stop her, well I never...So, whats next?'

'Lottie Allister's death was perpetrated in Glasgow, by those associated with Nick Diplock. So, to me, Edinburgh is not on my radar, it is Kenny, I want to see him again as he was not fulfilling with the whole truth.'

During dinner Isbel talked about her adventure in France, what had been said about, to what Jacklyn had witnessed. Denny and Jim had seen the Video Interview, so were agreeing to what Isbel was translating to. Isbel, was also dropping hints that Kenny was not telling the truth, was wondered where he could be. She was playing it casually, hoping they would pick up on it and do a search. All this time Isbel looked as though she was just enjoying the meal, that this was just typical dinner time banter.

Isbel, had realised, Jim loves delving into anyway he could stretch his prowess off computer knowledge, To Jim it was to him the challenge finding the whereabouts of someone at random. This is what he loved to do, for to Jim it better than playing a game of Chess.

Isbel smiled to herself, seeing the glint in Jim's eyes.

After dinner Isbel joined in with Denny and Jim, as Jim trolled the internet airways. Looking for any of Kenny's bad habits, Isbel was just getting tired when Jim did an air grab, he had found Kenny by the apps that he was using on his phone. He had used his phone to lay bets on dogs and horse racing; The IP address number indicated where he was in Glasgow, the map pinpointing precisely where. Isbel, already knew the address, did not need to write it down.

Isbel stretched her arms. 'I'm tired, I am going to bed. Night everyone.' Isbel was tired, and sleep, was what she needed.

***

The morning had more than a damp feel to it, the heavens had opened its sluice gates, the rain was bucketing down. Isbel looked fresh, was in a buoyant mood. Lottie had felt the vibes, the light-hearted way, Isbel was behaving. 'Have you something planned for the day Isbel?'

'Yes to the gym, I need to step up and get myself in shape. I spent to much time sitting about in France.'

Lottie knew Isbel had plans, Kenny was on Isbel radar, sooner or later she will hone in on him. Lottie also knew, Kenny was in trouble big time, did she want to stop Isbel? No, and yes. Lottie felt slightly confused for in a way she did not condone violence, yet she knew to try and stop Isbel was not going to work either, this is how Isbel needed to get this sorted, knowing in around about way, would get her's and Denny's life back to some normality. Lottie bit her lip, she also worried if something terrible would happen to Isbel, would she have the guilt on her conscience for evermore, the cold shiver she felt was nothing to do with the weather.

The Micra pulled into Craighall Industrial Estate where Pete's Gym was situated. Isbel's step was as meaningful as the purpose she was there for.

Pete looked up as she passed his office, the smile broadened on his face. Pete dropped doing the books, something more worthwhile had just entered. Texting Mags, proceeded to get the gym up and running. The early morning wave of office workers, who come to get themselves motivated before arriving at work by Nine, had just gone, it was that quiet spell before the next surge of the mums. Mags and the mums were soon there, as they entered the gym, the intense work out Isbel had set herself was in full swing. The mums just watched, their voices kept to a murmur, not to disturb Isbel. The punch bag was rocking with the flurry of kicks and punches that this Amazon of a girl was directing at it. Pete always seems to know when he had to get behind the punch bag, to give it support and when to step back. The mums looked exhausted just watching Isbel going through her paces, there was no stopping isbel, then the wind-down, not to stress the body, then into her ballet poses, stretching getting herself in control of her own body.

The coffee tasted good, as the mums gathered around to listen to Isbel. They wanted to know the hows and the wherefors, preferly what she had been directly involved in.

Isbel kept much back, just told them enough to keep them on her side. Her plans were simple, Kenny knew more than he had said, he was the one that could lead her to who murdered Allister. During the conversation with the mums, one mum informed Isbel that there was a place she could park the van, that was near to where she was staying with Lottie and Denny. So when the session was finished the mum Liza, drove the Micra to the secluded area, Isbel followed in the van. The spot was ideal. It had much cover, a large Oak and a few Beech trees. Amongst many Fir trees, and Holly Bushes inclued within a thick hedge to fields, a tractor track that led up to it. So, would not be easily spotted, not even if a helicopter flew over. Isbel's look of satisfaction pleased Liza, as it felt she was helping Isbel in her quest to avenge her brother's death. This was where Liza sometimes walked her dog and knew how secluded it was.

Lottie heard Isbel enter, her outstretched hand that reached out in Isbel direction, meant Lottie needed to talk. So, Isbel took her hand and led her to her bedroom. Once inside the bedroom, then seated on the side of the bed.

'I am so worried Isbel, this is getting to a point where there will be no turning back.'

Isbel cuddled Lottie. 'I'm afraid that the moment of Allister death, this was going to happen. I am not the person to turn my back on it, or give forgiveness. As you know, Allister was my twin brother, when he died, half of me died with him. I cannot be whole until I have had my revenge for Allister. Even if it means taking that person or persons, fighting all the way to hell, and staying there. Though, I must vent my revenge on those that actually did the deed, that is why I seek the truth. Last night before I went to sleep I wrote out my Will. So, all that what I own, goes to one person, that will need it. I just need two people to sign it as a witness. And I'm going there this afternoon, just to do that.'

'So this is what you wish, Isbel.'

'No, not wish, Lottie this is what I must do. I would not be able to live with myself, knowing I did nothing.'

Lottie had noticed the way Isbel had said 'nothing' there was that bite to it, like a snake attack, with much venom to it.

The drive to Glasgow was in daylight. Isbel entered through Paisley, then over the Erskine Bridge to Old Kilpatrick keeping clear of most of the traffic control cameras. This would lead her to where Kenny was, Duntocher. Her baggy clothes and baseball cap gave her the look of a delivery driver. As she parked the van a little way from where Kenny was staying? The little bag of steel ball bearings fitted neatly into her fist, this will give her introduction some weight to it. The small parcel and clipboard set the disguise. She rang the bell and waited. She could hear talking, then the door latch turned.

'Who is it?'

'Delivery for Miss J Nesmith.'

Isbel heard the safety chain being released, and the door started to open. The punch caught Janet entirely by surprise, with the help of Isbel. Janet slipped to the floor without making any noise

The television was on, the horse race was into its final half furlong, the noise was deafening as Kenny was on his feet, willing his horse on to victory. Arms in the air in a victory dance he turned, then with an almighty crash Kenny hit the television, they both, he and the TV crumbled to the floor. The chair was still in Isbel's hands, as she stood over him. She had no reason for concern, he was out like a light.

When Kenny came too, Janet was trussed up like a Chicken ready for the oven, He was completely naked, secured to the chair with ducktape. Then a dishcloth was pushed into his mouth. The realisation who was sitting in front of him, and who's cold eyes were directed straight at him, sent a cold sense of foreboding through his whole body, as it started to tremble at what Isbel would do to him.

'It seems you did not give me the full account of what had happened Kenny. Silly boy. I gave you the chance to inform me. yet you decided that was not what you wanted.'

Isbel had made sure she was fully protected, wearing clothes that would not give out any DNA samples. Wearing latex gloves under her fingerless training mitts, so as not to leave any fingerprints, on anything that would be left behind. Then taking out of the parcel she had brought with her, an electric soldering iron which she plugged into the nearest power point. Then as it heated, Isbel checked Janet's blindfold. turning the music up on the headphones, that Isbel had taped to Janet's ears. The uncooked chicken breast, Isbel had taken from the fridge was on a plate, so Kenny could see it. With the soldering iron hot, she tested it on the piece of chicken. The sizzling sound it made and the smell of burning it produced, Kenny knew what Isbel intention were. Isbel took the rag from his mouth.,

'I didn't kill him.'

The panic in his voice, the urine flowing down from the chair had no effect on Isbel.

'He came to you for help, and you did that to him.' Isbel lunged the rag back into Kenny's mouth, then pushed the soldering iron into Kenny's midriff. The muffled scream as she let the soldering iron burn into him. Taking the hot iron away, when Kenny seemed more subdued, she took the rag from his mouth. 'Well, what have you to say?'

Kenny's sobbing words came out more as a slobber. 'I had to Isbel, if they knew I had helped him they would have done the same to me.'

Isbel thrust the rag back into Kenny's mouth, then used the hot soldering iron again on him but left it there a bit longer. Kenny's body trembled heavely with the pain. Isbel turned her head and checked Janet, she too was shaking but was okay. When Isbel took the rag out off Kenny's mouth.

'No more Isbel, Please no more.'

Isbel looked at Kenny with contempt. 'Who torture Allister?'

Kenny did not hold back. 'Robert Burke, Gordon Burns and the Colombian, Jose.'

'And how do you know this?'

'They made us watch, it was to be a warning to us all what to expect if we stepped out of line.'

Isbel's anger was boiling up inside of her, then like a piranha fish on a feeding frenzy, she attacked Kenny. Leaving him still alive, but in a terrible mess, checking she had not left any evidence. As she exited the flat, she pulled the headphone cable out off the stereo player, that was attached to Janet's head, with the sound up high, coming out of the stereo's speakers. Isbel then left the flat, and walked towards the van and drove off.

The noise from the stereo soon had the local resident's attention, Police and Ambulance services where called.

Tom Burns received the message of the assault of two persons, indicating it was the address at Duntocher, that had his full attention. Tom Burns phone call, to his brother Gordon. 'She's here, in Glasgow.'

When Alex Burke eventually looked around the flat. He had to be careful; forensic were already there when he arrived, many photos had already been taken of the crime scene, Though he looked around carefully, it would not be possible to plant something of Isbel's, to implicate her, even though he was knowing she had commit the assult. Tom Burns was doing the knocking on the doors, trying to put words into people mouths, though he too, was finding he was getting nowhere, for nobody had seen anything to report.

As Isbel, was well acquainted with this area, with all the CCTV camera that were scattered about, she had left the way she came in. Isbel kept to her strict rules to drive sedately not too close to any vehicle in front of her, so she did not make herself noticed. The drive back to Musselburgh allowed her to evaluate her achievements and how the villains would react, knowing she was treading on their shirt tails.

She parked the van, then cleaned herself up, walked back to the house. Lottie was, relieved to see her. 'How did it go?'

'Great had coffee and a long chat, when the Will was signed, I came home.'

Denny was listening to the police messages of the attack at Duntocher. Then he had picked up the news broadcast on how one person was found tortured and was rushed to hospital with severe injuries. The news broadcaster, then went on to comment that the burn marks of a hot poker on the victim, this was similar to the murder of Allister Jordan. Jim looked at the address that's funny that where we found Kenny's IP address.

Lottie could hear them discussing the case, she had already put two and two together. Yet Isbel Jordan had left Kenny alive, thinking to herself. In a way, it was right that Isbel had not killed him, then she said to herself. 'It's still not right.' Lottie was in a dilemma, she knew it was not right, still knowing she could not tell anybody. The arm that cuddled Lottie was gentle. Isbel had seen the look on Lottie's face, knew she was struggling with her thoughts.

'The Bible says, an eye for an eye. The Law says, we must not take the law into our own hands. If the Law turns a blind eye, then someone has to help the law to see its failings.'

'But Isbel, two wrongs don't make a right.'

'That is true Lottie. But I was brought up with, 'Do unto those, that would do unto you.'

'Fight fire, with fire, we all get burnt? Isbel, please don't let it be you.'

'Lottie, this will rattle a few cages. Now I wait, let them get drawn into a false security, then strike again. I know the names of those that did it, not one but three. So the cauldron has to be big, to take its offerings to hell. And that is where they are going.'

Isbel kissed Lottie on the cheek. 'But which one, will be first?' Then casually. 'What we cooking? I'm hungry.'

Lottie turned on Isbel. 'How can you say that, after what has happened?'

'Lottie, they had fun doing what they did to Allister. Though if their Lawyer,s had their way, those bastards would plead their human rights, then ask for pity, will no doubt receive it. Well! What a pity, I won't be giving them any pity. But I can honestly say I won't be having fun, nor will I be enjoying it. This has to be done, this is like completing a mission. It has to be treated with respect, to make sure I get it right.'

Lottie knew it was no good her trying to persuade Isbel, knowing full well this was a crusade she was on, a mission to right the wrongs done to her brother. So, to try and get her mind away from it, Lottie decided to start preparing for dinner.

As Lottie peeled the potatoes, the thoughts were still there. 'I understand what you are saying Isbel, but it still feels wrong.'

Isbel, slicing the onions. 'After my experience with the Glasgow Police, I still have faith in the Police force in general, Yet these criminals can still slip in, then slip out while the police have their hands tied by legalities. That these criminals seem to think that it is something they have not to worry about.'

The voice of Denny butted into their conversation. 'Isbel we have agents working in Glasgow, sorting out who is who, They are building up a case against Burke and Burns. Don't tread on their toes otherwise, you might find yourself on that list. What I have come to say, Major Dupree has managed to find out from Jacklyn the name of the sloop. Jim as now started to put it in a program to keep tabs on its present situation, so we can track its whereabouts.'

After dinner, Denny wanted Isbel to see what they had achieved. Isbel sat between Denny and Jim, watching the evidence they were coordinating between MI5 and the CIA. Now with the agents from Interpol joining the fray, it was now upping the pace of the operations. Javi joining in with Denny and Jim, coordinating the data and cross-checking the evidence. This has given the operation a new impetus.

Jim pointing to how they can now direct the different teams to areas of the action, that was more relevant. 'Each group are finding out various information, and we can now formulate the strength of evidence that we are all sharing together. As circumstances change, we can help, by directing the right groups to the right targets, so none of the Agents is treading on each other toes. Yet keeping up to date with what they need to know, at first hand. Of course, the American's want to know what they want to know, with how it would affect America. Interpol much the same and the consequence it would have in Europe. Javi has given us vital information, they have gained by those who were involved chasing Jacklyn Kennedy. Where the latest information from Glasgow is that the incident with Kenny has caused ripples. Feathers seem to be ruffled, there is a certain feeling of discord amongst the gang members. Bickering has been seen to be happening with the gang leaders, Trust amongst them is becoming strained. Yet Burke and Burns, still seem to be holding their end up, and have carried on as usual.'

Isbel's thoughts were drifting about inside her head. 'Not for much longer, Burke will soon lose his cool, after what I got in store for him.' Isbel sat looking as though she was impressed with what Jim was saying. But in a way she was, for inadvertently Jim was giving her the information she needed.

At Glasgow's, Stewart Street Police Station, Burke and Tom Burns needed to evaluate how they could manipulate the evidence, so Isbel was involved. 'There is nothing here Tom, all that we can go on, is a man leaving the scene. This was given to the reporter of the Milngavie Herald by a nieghbour. Tom, we have to look at the evidence given to us by forensic's, for that is all we have for now. What makes it worse is that the boot print, forensic found inprinted on Dalrymple's chest was a size nine. The boot is of the type you can buy at any Builders Merchants. We know from the shoes that Isbel has left at her apartment that her shoe size is seven and a half. What we have is nothing.' Alex Burke got up from his chair and paced the floor.

Tom Burns carried on sitting on the corner of Burke's desk. 'So where is she, the last sighting of her we had, was when she attacked Kenny at his flat in Edinburgh… then nothing. Until now, she must have been given help?' Tom Burns picked up the folder that they had both compiled together trying hard to find Isbel, but it held no more information that they already knew. 'We both know what she is capable of.'

Burke spun round. 'You don't have to remind me, Tom. I have to see Robert's face every day for that. He was a good-looking lad, now he looks grotesque.' Burke kicked out at the filing cabinet. 'We have asked all forces to give us information, nothing has come to light, yet the Bank where she drew three thousand pounds from, at Dunbar, had said she had mentioned going south.' Alex Burke sat down in his chair and clasped his face with his hands. 'She must have ditched her car somewhere Tom, for her not to have been noticed.'

Chapter 10.

First in the bag.

Isbel stretched her arms. 'I'm tired, I'm off to bed.' Denny looks at the time, Nine forty-five. Isbel left them and went to say goodnight to Lottie. With her arm gently wrapped around Lottie's shoulder, giving her a gentle hug and a kiss. 'See you in the morning.'

Lottie reached up and touched Isbel hand. 'Yes, in the morning.'

Later as Lottie went to bed, she looked in on Isbel. She could hear the steady breathing and lowered her hand to feel the warmth of her body. Lottie felt relieved Isbel was sleeping, As she hated the thought that Isbel would go out late at night, and do those terrible things. But she knew Isbel had a strong reason for doing what she was doing.

As Lottie laid in bed next to Denny, the thoughts of being safe with him being there. Though Isbel would be on her own, was that the reason she did not like Isbel going out in the still of the night on her own? Then with those thoughts in her head, she drifted into sleep.

Isbel was already up and moving around. Wearing the thick black clothes and tennis shoes. She opened the window and with small egg-shaped balls of blue tac Isbel attached the blue tac to the corners of the sash window, then to the cockspur handle, so it did not drop and lock her out. Then eased herself out into the night, closing the window onto the blue tac, so the window seemed closed. Then taking the same route into Glasgow, as she had done when she confronted Kenny. She had learnt from watching the work Denny and Jim, had been showing her that night, who was living where and their habits. Robert Burke was a creature of habits, Isbel also knew Glasgow like the back of her hand, She was taking full advantage of it. Isbel was heading for Robert Burke's favourite drinking hole, his regular meetings with Greer and Erskine was well known, with the timing it was perfect. Isbel parked up near where Burke lived, she pulled the thick socks over her tennis shoes, then with a little struggle she pushed her feet into the size nine boots. She needed a tight fit, so they did not become awkward for her to wear. Then Isbel walked to where Greer, Erskine and Robert would be together. Finding a dark place to wait, she put on the fingerless training mitts she used on the punch bag, so that she did not show any damage, to the knuckles on her fist. She was now ready.

Robert Burke was ready to leave, Greer and Erskine jokingly saying to him. 'Watch out for the shadows, for the black widow spider.'

Robert Burke waved his hand and laughed. 'Fock off...see ya.' As he went through the door into the night air, pulling his jacket collar up, looked around just in case, nodded with a smile on what they had inplied. He shoved his hands into his trouser pockets and sauntered home. The ten-minute walk would do him good, he thought to himself. He did not notice the tall, dark figure that used the shadows to conceal herself.

Robert Burke arrived at his home, as he approached his front door, bent his head down to see where he was putting the key, with his one good eye. Isbel struck, her punch was aimed at the top of the nape at the back of his neck. His head hit the door with a thunderous crash.

Isbel picked him up, carried him over her shoulder, in a firemans lift. towards the LDV van. Deposited him into the back of the van closing the doors behind her, then with plenty of Ducktape, she secured him. Then drove back to Musselburgh, parked the van, checked that Robert had no way of moving, locked the van. Then headed back to the bungalow, to her bed.

***

Lottie entered Isbels bedroom, Isbel was still asleep. Taking a deep sigh, Lottie went to the kitchen to make the morning tea. She was deep in thought as she went through with her morning routine. Being blind had its disadvantages, but blind and alone, had been to her a nightmare. The night terrors she went through until she met Denny had been history, now she was beginning to have them again. Not that she felt insecure in herself, more to what would happen to Isbel if she had got it all wrong, finding herself in the hands of those terrible people. This was what worried her more than anything else, She had become to love Isbel being around her, she was beginning to accept her as a younger sister of some sort. Now the worry of losing her was becoming her biggest fear. Then the sense of someone being there, Lottie relied on her greatest asset her nose. 'Morning Isbel.'

Isbel's crocky voice. 'Morning Lottie, I slept so well, that my mouth now is so dry, I need a drink.' Lottie poured out a cup and gave it to her. 'Thank you Lottie, you are a treasure.' Then Isbel sat down at the kitchen table.

'What are your plans today Isbel?'

'I have a job to consider Lottie and need to keep in shape. To sit around and do nothing will not help me long term. I am going down to the gym and have a good long work out. There is nothing I can do that would push this along without upsetting someone. So, the punch bag, is where I can imagine, it is one of those I would love to vent my anger on. That should give me the work out I require.'

Lottie had heard Isbel say the same things before, yet Isbel somehow seemed to do something that was disconcerting to others peoples point of view, which caused people to worry about her mental attitude. For it was how Lottie saw it, Isbel had complete control of how to handle all situations. She knew what was right and wrong, as her feeling towards others showed she did care about their feelings, Isbel had respect for others around her. Lottie needed to get away from her thoughts she was having, trying to look at a brighter image. The sound of Jim Anderson brought her mind back into focus, Jim had got up early to catch up on the nights developments.

'The report from the Police about the attack on Kenny said a man was responsible, as the prints found on the scene gave proof that it was a man. Please accept my apologies Isbel, I thought it was you.'

DCI Burke had released the report, believing it might make Isbel think she was safe. Hoping it would make Isbel careless. But it also was a calculated gamble on his behalf to look as though he was only acting on the evidence that had been presented.

Denny came through the doorway. 'What's this.' As he heard the news report.

Jim told Denny about the police statement. But Denny's reaction showed his disbelieve in the truth of the report. For he knew that Isbel had done it. How? That did not matter, for Isbel had covered her tracks. Because as Denny had read it, that it had helped to push the operation forward. It had not hampered it. The look he gave Isbel then the wink. This gave Isbel the knowing, that Denny knew. Isbel did not respond back, just in case it jeopardised what her aims were in the first place. She too, was treading a fine line also knew, she still had to be careful.

After breakfast, Isbel set off for the gym, first, she must check on the condition of Robert Burke. The bruise on his forehead was evident of his contact with his head hitting the door and needed checking. As Isbel opened the back of the van, Robert's eyes met Isbel's, the terror in his eyes confirmed his worse fears. Isbel pulled at the duck tape that covered his mouth, slowly until just a corner of his mouth showed, then from her bag she took a length of six millimeters of soft plastic tubing then gently inserted into his mouth, replaced the duck tape sealing the tube so it could not fall out. The other end of the tubing she placed into a large water container. Robert sucked on the tube and spluttered for sucking too hard. She took the pipe out off the bottle and cut a bit off of it, replaced the remaining length of tubing back into the bottle, then peeled back the duck tape from the other side of Roberts' mouth, then again gently inserted the short piece of tube through his lips, replacing the tape. Robert found by using his tongue he could control which tube he needed. That done Isbel secured the Van and headed for the Gym. The way Isbel acted was, as normal as any other mornings work out, those at the gym had no idea what she had done or what she was about to do.

On the Glasgow streets, much was the same. People were carrying on as usual. But Nick Diplocks men were looking for Robert Burke, he had not shown up where he should have been.

Jim Anderson keeping an eye on developments in Glasgow was seeing some concerns, could not relate to it, did not know what was being played out. He brought Denny's attention towards it. 'What you reckon?'

Denny watched the footage. Sending a message to the MI5 agent, asking what was happening. The agent sounded that he was not sure, but would keep a close eye on the situation.

Denny was involved with what was happening in Edinburgh. Jim was monitoring the movement of the sloop that was sailing in the inner sea of the Western Isles. The Satellite picture was so clear he could see all those on deck, then a small boat moored up alongside the sloop, with people that were being taken onboard, Jim took snapshots so he could pass on the information, back to the authorities. The CIA was now contacting Jim, and a three-way conversation was being had between GCHQ, MI5 and CIA. On what was proceeding. It was late in the afternoon when Denny had a reply from the MI5 agent in Glasgow. 'There seems to be some concern about the whereabouts of Robert Burke. That's the word we are getting from the street.'

Isbel was still at the gym, Pete and Mags were working with a group of disabled persons. Isbel was helping them, getting involved. This had taken her mind off what was happening elsewhere. Isbel loved these handicapped peoples sense of humour, so when a teenage girl suffering from a rare genetic condition explained to Isbel in a distorted manner, that she was also like a trainer. 'I have to tell my carer's, how to look after me, it's like teaching dogs to jump through a hoop.' Then she laughed. 'It's harder for me because I can't crack a whip.' The little chuckle she gave as her fascial twitchess gave her head little jerking movement as she laughed, Isbel just could not help laughing to herself, gave the girl a gentle hug.

This was to Pete and Mags, the beneficial side of their work. Pete was most appreciative with Isbel's help ' Isbel, after these unfortunate persons have been sitting about for very long periods, these exercises can help these disabled persons to stimulate some of their muscles, getting their circulation working. We must appreciate, that to these disabled persons, it still going to be hard work for them, for just being able to be here. This will gives them something completely different, then for them just sitting around.'

Later Isbel dropped by a local grocers shop and picked up some cans of soup and a tin opener, then to the van, Robert could not move and looked at her despairingly. She opened a can of tomato soup, took the tubing out of the water container and put it in the soup can. Isbel sat and watched him suck on the tube, seeing the red soup being drawn up into his mouth. Then now and again would change the tube to the water then back to the soup. When she left him, she had made sure he had water to drink.

Lottie hearing Isbel, chirped up. 'I'm in the kitchen Isbel.' Isbel came in, Lottie could smell the tomato soup, lingering on Isbel. 'Have you had a good day Isbel?'

Isbel told Lottie about her day with the disabled people, and the fun they had together. Let alone the laughs, from the comments when these handicapped persons talked about the predicament that they found themselves in, always relying on others. 'What joy it would be to pick my own nose, without poking my eye out, or being able to wipe my own arse.' Said one elderly man. Lottie knew the sentiment of their comments, gave a wry smile.

Jim was the last one sitting down to dinner he passed a report to Denny from the MI5 agent in Glasgow, which read. 'There seemed a lot of confusion about the disappearance of Robert Burke. He left Greer and Erskine at two-thirty in the morning, for the ten-minute walk home. There was blood on the door to his house, but no sign of him entering. A neighbour heard a noise and looked out of their window, saw a tall man carrying something. Then went back to bed.'

Denny looked at Isbel. 'This has your calling card attached to it.'

Isbel said nothing, carried on eating her dinner. She still had her plans, they were meant to upset the equilibrium of this gang of Nick Diplock's. Isbel's wanting for revenge, that hadn't changed, it was just how she was going to take it. Isbel had not made up her mind on how it would finish, that would depend on the circumstances at that time, in the final conclusion to this sordid affair.

It was after dinner that Isbel sat with Denny and Jim. It was mainly to see, what had appeared on the monitors, that were so concerning her? The images of Glasgow were of all the known places where the principal villains were holed up. Gordon Burns and Jose the Colombian that are occupying Isbel Flat. Two cameras that were now facing the block of flats. Both front and back elevation entrances, were covered, Isbel could not see any cameras pointing between the two buildings. Isbel brought up the layout in her mind. The two blocks of six-storey flats had a distance of seven feet between them, with a five-foot-high dividing wall separating the two properties. The windows that was on the side elevation were giving light only, to the stair landing that had only a single fanlight, but not big enough for her to get her body through. This side elevation was not covered by any of the cameras, there had been no need as there was no door openings on that elevation. The traffic cameras she had already noted where they were, so how does she get in and out without them knowing. Isbel went to bed to think and make plans.

Once again Lottie checked on Isbel before going to bed herself.

The morning light woke Isbel, the plan came to her while she slept. It was clear what she must do, even though would still have problems. One of them was the amout of spending money. If she drew out cash or paid by her credit card, she still could be traced. The equipment she needed would cost her more than she had left. Isbel showered and made her way to breakfast. Her brain could not stop working on her dilemma. Even when driving to the gym, before stopping to check on Robert Burke. He looked a little distressed, but was still alive. At the gym, she put in a significant shift, it was Sally, one of the mums, that she wanted to have a word with. After she had spoken with Sally, they agreed to a meet; the plan was still a possabilty. Isbel carried on until some time after the mums, had gone home. Then said goodbye to Pete and Mags. Drove straight to meet Sally, where she lived.

Sally had mentioned in a previous conversation, what she and her husband use to do as a hobby. Why Isbel needed to enquire was, had they still kept the equipment. The answer was yes, it was stored in Sally's Garage. Sally and her husband use to like rock climbing, after her husbands near miss climbing accident it had to stop. Sally had strongly laid it out to her husband when he was recouping from his injuries, that she did not want to end up being a single mum.

Sally opened the door of the garage and showed Isbel the full extent of the equipment: Harness, Belay, Cams, ascenders, pulleys and a extensive array of ropes. Isbel had done rock climbing before, even for the stunt work, was well aware of what was needed. Isbel was delighted to see that Sally had a three metre aluminium three pole diagonal braced gantry scaffold section, they had used for practising, now it was used to hold the equipment hanging from the garage ceiling. They loaded the climbing equipment into the Micra with the scaffold section pushed through the sunroof. Then Isbel drove to where the van was and loaded the van with the gear, just one more piece of the jigsaw.

Robert's eyes followed every move Isbel made, he had tried his damnedest to move, but the ducktape held fast. He could not bend his knees, or move a muscle as Isbel had secured him in a sitting position, as he felt like an Egyptian Mummy. The van his sarcophagus.

Isbel's plan was now workable, with a visit to a local hardware and tool shop, was a nessacary stop. When Isbel arrived back at the house, she had everything she needed.

Lottie was now more relaxed, the thought that it was not Isbel that had attacked Kenny, also was not connected to the disappearance of Robert Burke. Had given her new hope for Isbel. Even when she, spoke to Isbel, it was different, as it was not so solemn and concerning, has it had been these past few days.

After dinner, Isbel resumed her place with Denny and Jim. The MI5 agent was in his element. The search for Robert Burke by Diplock's men, had given them new places that MI5 did not know about, that the gang were using to store their drugs. So her plan was working she had pushed the operation along faster than it had been going. The cameras trained on the block of flats where Isbel apartment was being used by Gordon and Jose, showed no change. Isbel took great care to where the cameras were situated and what they could see, or more what they could not see.

Chapter 11.

She bagged a brace.

That night Isbel waited for Lottie to check up on her, then she was up and raring to go. She drove into Glasgow at about Two in the morning, on the A721 through into Tollcross, cutting through side streets to avoid the cameras. Parked the van at the rear car park to the block of flats, next to her flat, then used the lock picks to enter the rear doors. She carried the equipment up to the top foor, onto the flat roof, through the service door. Setting up the pulleys with the rope and tackle above the landing windows, attached to the scaffold section, Isbel spanned the two buildings with the scaffold section sitting on two old cushions she had secured to the gantry preventing them from sliding and falling off, this would stop the platform from slipping and making a noise. Isbel lowered four ropes down the side of the building, two of the lines attached to pulleys. Then abseiled down to the window that was situated directly at the stair landing that led to the entrance door of her apartment. The PVC window was of the first type made, that had the glazing beads on the outside and not the inside. Attaching the three suction grip pads to the glass, and securing the ropes to them. Isbel now removed the glazing beads with the specialist tool she bought at the tool shop, placed the glazing beads in the rope bucket attached to one off the ropes, then with her legs spread out, with her feet firmly placed on the brickwork of the flats either side of the window, then with a large tug on the suction pads, breaking the seal...removed the glass. Then pulling on the ropes, she lifted the double glazed unit up above the opening, securing it in position, allowing it to hang down on the side of the building. Now she was inside the building, using a little mirror attached to a bent down wire clothes hanger, Isbel gently slid it through the letter plate, she was now able to see inside the flat checking the security latch was not being used on the door. It was quiet, using her key she entered, checking the first bedroom which would have been Allister's bedroom. Jose was fast asleep on the bed. Then checking her own bedroom, Gordon was also sleeping. Isbel checked the kitchen, as she went to leave the kitchen, she notices a syringe and a small packet with some white powder beside the cutting board, dabbing her finger onto it, tasted the Cocaine, things were getting better.

Isbel thoughts were now of how she had found out that her parents were injecting Cocaine And seeing them make the solution, that they needed to be able to inject themselves with the drugs. That was when she was almost Sixteen still attending school. Then that morning when her father accused her of selling her body, lashing out at her. She fought back with the anger she was feeling inside that her father could believe the lies that Burke and Burns had spread about her. Isbel speed of action and of the pentup anger that raged inside her, she had soon overpowered her father, seeing him laying there, she made a strong cocaine solution and injected it into the vein in his arm. leaving him there, calmly left the house to attend school as if nothing had happened. The Death Certifitcate said he had overdosed. To Isbel her father was the cause of her mother addiction, now it was one less problem for her to worry about, it could make her mother give up her dependency on the drugs. That never happened, her mother just gave up, six months later Isbel's mother did overdose.

Now setting up a solution to fill the syringe with the Cocaine, Isbel went back to Jose. Using some short lengths of rope, she placed them under, and up over the bed, the first to secure his legs the second his arms and body. Setting up slipknots she was ready the pull on the ropes to tie him to the bed, the struggle he gave was short lived as Isbel struck him, her training mitts making sure she left no trace of bruising to her knuckles. Then the duck tape over his mouth kept him quiet. Then she injected some of the Cocaine into the vien in his neck. Making sure he was secured. She listened for Gordon, it was quite, he was okay, back to Jose, his eyes were scurrying about yet not focused on anything. The Cocaine was taking effect. Now for Gordon.

The noise she that she now heard was Gordon Burns using the bathroom. Standing concealed in the bedroom doorway where Jose was trusted up on the bed, Isbel checked the training mitts that she wore on her hands, she waited. Gordon had not gone back to bed he was in the lounge, she did not panic, just waited. The syringe was still half full of the Cocaine solution, Isbel was waiting for the right opportunity. She waited till Gordon Burn's back was towards her, the move she made was silent yet instantaneous, there was no stopping Isbel when a job was to be done. The heel of her builders boot caught Gordon at the base of the spine, as he hit the floor, he was turning to defend himself. Grabbing at Isbel foot as she tried to take a kick at his head, trying hard to get a hold, only able in twisting her foot. Isbel went with the momentum of the twist, then rolling to her feet in one clean movement. Gordon tried to get to his feet but Isbel's first strike had done damage, the pain in his back hampered his progress as the next attack was already on its way. Her boot aimed at his windpipe missed grazing his chin as the foot skimmed up his face, connecting to his nose pushing the nose bone upwards. Isbel was already twisting her body to keep clear of any free hand that Gordon might have, to make her life uncomfortable. As he fell back, he laid where he landed, in pain, clutching his face. Isbel delivered the next blow to his temple, Gordon laid motionless, she emptied the rest of the contents of the syringe into him. Then secured him with Duck tape. Now she could concentrate on Jose, in the same way. When she was satisfied with her efforts of making sure they could not move, Isbel carried them one at a time, to the stair landing. She secured the bodies with ropes, pushed them one at a time through the appiture, lowered him down to the ground to otherside block of flats from the landing window. Checking the flat she had left nothing there to incriminate herself, secured the entrance door. Connecting the next body hung it just under the window, she will use him as a platform for herself to replace the glazing panel back in position, fixing the glass back into postion, again with the glazing beads using a thick piece of cloth to deaden the impact as she hammered the glazing beads with a soft headed hammer, she then cleaned the window, so the marks of the suction pads did not show, lowered herself down on the last body to the ground. Where she could dispatch the two bodies to the van. Isbel needed to collect the equipment together entering the other block of flats as she had previously done, dropped all the climbing gear to the ground, cleaned the roof of any evidence, she secured the entrance door to the roof. Gathering everything together, loaded it into the van. She made her way back to Musselburgh, arriving back just in time, just before they all woke up

***

Robert could make out the two bodies that were keeping him company, that made him worry more. For they too, were trusted up just as he was, he could not move a finger, nor could they. Laying there, like a spiders meal wrapped up in the spider's sticky web thread, waiting for their life fluids to be sucked from them.

Isbel had a sense of achievement, she had those that tortured Allister. Now she had the power of revenge. First, she must act like a good girl behaving herself. Her thoughts were confirming to herself how she felt. 'Yes, I can do that, now I can, I've all the time in the world. But first I must act normally. I don't want anyone to get in the way of my duty to Allister.' The sense of relief now eased through her body, a sigh as her breathing slowed down to a more stable rate, as she laid in bed waiting for Lottie to check up on her.

A shower helped to freshen her up, and at breakfast, she looked okay.

Her visit to the van to check on her new house guest, just to keep them alive. Isbel was going to make sure, that they knew what they had done, that they were not going to go unpunished. The look on Robert's face as Isbel opened the van door, expecting the worst. But Isbel just removed the ropes and tackle and placed them in the Micra. Checking on Jose his eyes were closed, she slapped his face, his eyes sprang open the red glare in them showed the Cocaine was still doing it's worst, as it was with Gordon. Robert still had plenty of water, so she left them to it, locking the van and heading for Sally's Garage. This was to give back the climbing equipment and a extra hundred pounds for sally's benefit. Then to the gym, there was no workout planned for to day, she explained her night activities as a reckie trying to find out where they could all be. The coffee with the mums, helped to keep her eyes open.

Then it was back to the van to check up on the hostages, with that completed it was back to Lottie. By nine that evening, Isbel was fast asleep in her bed.

***

The morning was hectic there had been new developments. Jim was scanning all the cameras. Denny was with him. Isbel could see Jim was frantic, he just kept muttering. 'How the bloody hell did they do that?'

'What has happened Jim?' As if Isbel knew nothing of it.

'All day, MI5 has kept a close eye on your flat. The suspects did not behave as normal, so this morning they checked inside. They were gone, but how? The cameras picked up nothing. They did not leave the building. There were signs of a struggle in the lounge. Now Nick Diplock's men are worrying, they are looking over there shoulders at each other. Alex Burke is pacing his office shouting abuse at Tom Burns.'

Denny lent back in his chair, and with a searching voice. 'I don't know how you did it Isbel, but it is, bloody well working.'

Isbel touched his shoulder, then bent forward and kissed him on the cheek.

Jim, looking on in a bemused way, his thoughts were confused, 'how could a girl take out two men of their description on her own?' He now had to stop thinking to himself. For Jim had more pressing matter at hand, the Sloop was now in a position for action to be taken. The satellite camera that was plotting its course had identified Nick Diplock. He was now on board the sloop. They now have him in connection with a crime being committed. Nick Diplock was finding it hard to recruit men, was having to pull his sleeves up and to muck in. This is not how Isbel had planned it at first, but with her action of creating confusion with Nick Diplock's men. It became the reason for what was happening now.

Isbel still had to hold fire until she was sure that Burke and Burns were not escaping from justice. MI5 had set the trap, with the Special Task Force, that were waiting in the wings for their cue to step in. Stewart Street, unaware of what was unfolding. The action was already taking place in Edinburgh. The business had been concluded, with the various Crime Organisations were now packing up to go home. It was now time for those International Law Enforcement Team to select, and to make decisions on who to arrest, and who to just follow up on. There was the need to confirm, on how these villains had entered the Country undetected.

Isbel sat with Lottie for a late breakfast, of toast with lots of melting butter and thick cut Marmalade, with a large mug of strong coffee. Isbel needed to check her house guest, but at this moment in time, it could wait. She could hear the excited talking Denny and Jim were having over the arrest of the Sloop. A Royal Navy Frigates Crew, had boarded the Sloop in the sound of Jura, close to the Isle Gigha, was now heading for the Dock where they will catch any other member of Nick Diplocks Gang that would be waiting. It was just three of them that were waiting at the dock, they were soon rounded up and taken into custody.

Still, Alex Burke was free, MI5 had not enough to arrest him including Tom Burns, they needed more evidence. MI5 was not content with them having just a slap on the wrist, they were more interested, for them to get a much stiffer sentence. Isbel was still keeping an eye on the proceedings. She knew Alex Burke had always kept his powder dry, now once again he had covered his tracks, and looked as though he was going to wriggle off the hook once again.

DCI Burke was making phone calls, he was putting pressure on all his informants. His unusual iratic behaviour was upsetting DS Burns. 'Look Alex, settle down. Isbel will show her hand soon, mark my words, then we can silence her forever.' DS Burns was not happy, it was not going to plan, as Alex's behaviour was not helping. Losing their nerve at this stage was not how they always covered their tracks.

Chapter 12.

Revenge.

The bodies were alive, but not kicking, when she opened the van door. She checked their bindings and replaced a fresh water container. Then Isbel put some tubing into Gordon and Jose's mouths the same as she had done for Robert. Wanting them alive, when she finally executes her revenge on them. Isbel had put some sodium lactate in with the water. Isbel did not know what she was going to do eventually, but she wanted to keep her option open for now. Alex Burke and Tom Burns were in this together, if it had only been one of them that had been involved in the torture of Allister, it still did not excuse them both from this.

Pete and Mags were helping the mums with a keep fit exercise class when Isbel joined them, They found it funny having Isbel doing the same as them. It also showed that the exercise suited everyone. Pete and Mags appreciated how Isbel joined in and was happy to see Isbel explain to the mums the benefits of it for them. Isbel also informed them that her mission was coming to a conclusion, that she would soon have to go back to work, thanked them for the help they had given her, putting to right, the wrongs that had been done to Allister and herself. Isbel knew it was coming to that moment of no return, good or bad she was going to have her revenge. Even if it cost her life as well. She could not accept living if she could not do that last deed for Allister. So, this was her way of saying thank you to them, even if it meant she did not return.

Isbel's surprise to see Erica sitting with Lottie and Denny in the lounge on her return. Erica's honey blonde hair pulled back into a short ponytail. With her no-nonsense, direct look, she portrayed. This was Erica's CIA look, but that soon melted seeing Isbel. Agent Jesmond Freeman was sitting with them. Isbel had not seen the Audi Q5, so it did not register that they were there.

The warm hug that Erica and Isbel gave each other showed the working relationship that they had between themselves. Sitting down, Erica explained why she was there. 'Isbel, Jesmond use to be my old partner, he contacted me when he realised you had been working for us. He informed me, that Fairfax believes you have been working on your own, They believe you have a Colombian somewhere, that the Bureau is interested in talking with.'

'How did they come to that conclusion?' A cold stare attached to Isbels comment.

Agent Freeman could not wait to explain, bending forward sitting on the edge of his seat. 'We have closely worked with all the International Organisation within this operation. Sharing very bit of intelligence at our disposal. Yet we have no idea how you did it, but we know you did. We have put our best Profilers on your case, each one has come up with the same conclusion, that you are the person more likely to have achieved kidnapping those three individuals. We have no proof to back up our suspicions. Isbel we want that Colombian alive.' Agent Freeman, looking straight at Isbel with a determined look; It was now, that he started to feel uncomfortable, for the look of Isbel's cold black piercing eyes, made him sit back in his chair. His Adam's apple lifting up as he gulped, he had never seen such coldness, it gave him the shivers.

Erica watched with interest how Jesmond reacted. 'Isbel, can we walk together?'

They both rose from their chairs, then headed for the rear garden. Erica needed to gain Isbel trust to remind her of what the situation Isbel could be finding herself in. 'That look, proved to me you have Jose.' Isbel did not try to hide from that statement, for a moment Isbel was quietly contemplating her next move.

'Those three tortured Allister, for four days. I will have my revenge. Jose is not a bargaining chip that the Americans can pay him for information then let him loose.'

'No, I can't guarantee that won't happen.'

'Then there is no more to be said, it's not going to happen.'

Erica understood Isbel, she did not condone it, knowing Isbel, she would not back down. Looking at Isbel with a severe expression. 'They won't take no for an answer Isbel, they will come for him, and you. You know that don't you?'

Isbel turned, the look she gave Erica. 'I see anyone that looks a likely threat, will be treated as someone to eliminate.'

This time it was Erica that paused, taking a deep breath, said nothing. She had read the profiles that Jesmond had shown her, it said in their conclusion.

Handle with caution, not to be dismissed lightly, Isbel will react instantly, with extreme violation. The part of the report on Kenneth Dalrymple. Whoever had perpetrated this act, had acted like a wild animal. Erica touched Isbel's arm, while looking into her face, nodded her acceptance of Isbel's meaning, turned and left the garden to speak with Jesmond.

Isbel paced the garden, Erica was right they would come and get him, that's what the Americans do. Its what they know they can do, other countries complain. America just ignores them. Like the bullies in the School Playground saying, so what are you going to do about it?

Erica shook her head at Jesmond. They gave their farewells and left the house. As they headed for Edinburgh. Erica spoke, You know she will kill anyone that approaches her, if she deemed them a threat.'

Jesmond nodded. 'It's not in my hands Erica, as you well know. Fairfax wants the Colombian at all cost.'

Isbel knew it was the time. The American's had the technology and the manpower to get their own way. She walked around the side of the house and sprinted using every cover she could, not knowing if the Americans had already a Satellite trace on her. She raced to the Van. Then slowly without taking any chance to be noticed, drove off in a sedate manner.

Isbel was heading for Glasgow but needed a couple of things to complete her mission. More petrol, then the fishing tackle shop would be the ideal place. Plastic buckets and cord then proceeded to the run down garage where this sordid affair started. The area was due for renovation, and many of the buildings were boarded up,

Isbel parked the van a short distance from the garage, she needed to locate the CCTV camera, that MI5 had installed. Isbel had a rough idea of the direction, from the images of the garage where the camera is directed at, so that was probably where the camera could be situated. They would not have placed it too high up, so to get a clear image of the faces. When Isbel discovered the whereabouts of the camera it had been set in putty on a window ledge, a pencil type camera which she covered over with the thick cloth she had used on the glazing beads.

Isbel then backed the van up to the doors of the garage. Picking the lock she was in, the dirty windows that had not been cleaned for years gave out a mirky light, she surveyed the interior and a plan formed in her head. The pole that Allister had been suspended on, was a three-metre scaffolding pole, Isbel could see the remanents of the rope that Allister was bound with, still attached to the pole. There were more poles scattered about including a rusty old bucket of scaffold clips and a spanner, that had been left there by the demolishing firm. It did not take Isbel long to set-up two more poles in place, side by side, three feet apart, Isbel snatched at them with her full weight to test them. She was satisfied.

Taking the first one of her hostages inside the building, Isbel laid the body of Jose's face down on the floor, then with a direct kick to his head bore him unconscious. She cut the clothes from him, and trust him up, almost as they had trusted Allister naked to the pole. Then proceed with the other two, in the same manner, each one close together. When Isbel had achieved that task, she tied the plactic buckets to their testicles with the cord.

The fear on their faces when they gained consciousness, did not concern Isbel. 'So you thought you could do what you liked, and get away with it?' Looking straight at Robert, Isbels cold eyes bore into him. 'Don't worry Robert, Daddy will be here for you.' Then turning to Gordan. 'As Robert's father will come, so will that moron of a brother of yours will be here too. I've booked you on a one-way ride to hell, I so hope you will enjoy it.'

Robert, Gordan and Jose tried as hard as they could to wriggle themselves free. But it was no good, the bonds held fast, then with lack of food, and with a forlorn sense of hopelessness, their will, just evaporated.

Then from the back of the van, Isbel collected the petrol cans, which she had filled one at a time, each time she had filled up at the garage. She then proceeded to quarter fill the buckets with the petrol. Placing as many rags as she could, some were the clothes Isbel had cut from her victims. With any rags and paper, then with bits of timber, which she found scattered around the garage. Two forty-gallon drums of old engine oil had been left there, adding the old used engine oil mix with the petrol, she made sure she doused everywhere around the inside of the garage. Under the bench, in the old office. Isbel found the main fuse box and checked the fuses. She only needed one fuse that was for the lighting circuit, everything was falling into place. Pulling at the conduit which held the flex down for the light, she now had the length of flex that was needed to placed the lightbulb into the middle bucket off the three buckets. Isbel then carefully twisted and removed the glass bulb just leaving the two pronge filiment intact, did not need to touch the petrol, for as soon as the switch is thrown it will ignite the petrol. It was all set up. Isbel calculated that the normal used engine oil garage smells, would mingle with smell of the petrol fumes. Isbel double checked herself before she flicked the switch back on the fusebox

Isbel looked all around, the run-down garage, she was looking at the sequence of events that would happen. The look of panic on all of Isbel victim faces as they watched Isbel, could see what was in store for them, they were useless to stop her. Isbel was waiting for the light to fade, so for the light switch to be used.

Pulling the doors of the garage shut and making them secure, she then drove the van away from the garage, then went back and took the cloth away from the CCTV camera. Returning to the van, Isbel had parked it in a place which was dark. She wanted to make sure she could see the eventual climax of her endeavours. From her bag, she retrieved a mobile phone, which belonged to Robert Burke. She had taken the battery out so it could not be traced. Now replacing the battery, she then texted. 'Dad I'm locked in the garage.' Taking the battery out again dropped the phone, down the nearest drain. Then waited.

Alex was at his desk when the text pinged and instantly called Tom Burns. The speed they travelled with their blue light flashing, did not take them long. They did not proceed with any precautions and made straight for the door. Tom Burns had the key ready to open the door. And they both burst in switching on the light as they went. The explosion shook the surrounding buildings, as flames engulfed the garage. Isbel watching did not see them come out. Knowing they had perished, slowly drove the van away from the area. As a second and bigger explosion was heard.

The drive back to Musselburgh, Isbel kept her speed steady as she did not need to be stopped or caught in a speed trap. Parking the van in its usual parking place, she proceeded to jog back to the house. Lottie heard her open the door and met her as she came in, the distinctive smell of petrol on Isbel meant only one thing.

'Have you done it?'

'Yes.'

Lottie gave a sigh. 'Now what?'

'I pack my bag and drive back to Glasgow, present myself to Stewart Street.'

Denny came in. 'How many?'

'Five.'

'That meaning Burke and Burns.'

'Yes.'

Lottie sat down. 'When'

'Now Lottie, its no good hanging it out.' With that Isbel took the keys to the Micra out of her pocket, returned them to Denny.

'You might feel that you were used, but I did tell you from the start. I would have my revenge on whoever did this to Allister.'

Lottie rose from her chair and held her arms out waiting for a hug.

Isbel with tears in her eyes, the delayed affect on what she had achieved for Allister, duly replied. 'Lottie, you would have been a good mum.'

Denny joined in, he did not want to be left out. He was having the feeling of being Isbel's guardian. 'Don't hang yourself, they have got no proof. So, say no more than you have to.' It spilled out, spoken much like from an overprotective parent.

Jim, looking on, did not know what to say. Slightly confused with himself, there was a feeling of awkwardness not knowing how he should respond. He started to raise his hand, then put it down again. But seeing his old friend going soft, about someone who has just disposed of five lives, without remorse; had left him in a state of confusion as to what was the right way to act.

Lottie followed after Isbel, as she went to gather her things together. Once they were in the bedroom, Isbel placed some clothes on to the bed, the rest into her bag, then looking at Lottie sitting on the bed, with tears streaming from her eyes. This brought home how much she was going to miss her and Denny. Sitting down next to Lottie, she could not contain the inner emotion she was having, with the vast hugging and sobbing between them, were of two people showing their true feelings towards each other.

'I've done what I have set out to do, Lottie. Now I must face those that have to judge if they agree with my action, or if they don't. Then if they don't, then I must be punished. Do I have regrets? Yes, because I found so many nice people here, who have supported me. Now it will be how the media report on what I have done, will be how many of them will judge me good or bad. Yet in a way I have protected them, from these bad people, will their conscience see it that way? Or will they feel, they have just been used?'

Denny who had been standing at the bedroom door, came and gave Lottie support and took her away from the bedroom. Isbel sat on the bed, for a moment reflected on those last few emotional feelings. Then she showered and changed her clothes, Isbel went to collect her bag. That is when she noticed the phone. Turning it on, there were no messages. Checking her contacts, she pressed Hugh McKeon. And to text the place he could collect the van, hinted it will need a spring clean. Then deleted him from the phone, staring down at the phone she keyed through all the messages. Then removed the sim card, then proceeded to say good-bye to them all. The phone, Isbel gave back to Denny, who instinctively returned her old phone back to Isbel.

'I've recharged the battery Isbel, there is nothing on there to incriminate you. Careful what you say, they have no evidence.' Denny still trying to protect her.

Isbel reversed the Audi A3 out of the garage, with her side window opened said. 'Bye, Love you both.' Set off for Glasgow. With many thought going through her head. As she drove, it was more of instinct, for she had no idea what was about to happen to her. She done what she had set out to do, she had no regrets.

Isbel's first stop was Steve's gym. The look on Steve's face seeing her was not of surprise but of pleasure. ' Isbel, come here, give me a hug.' Isbel's solemn look did not dampen his feelings. 'Come, let's talk it through over some coffee.'

Isbel proceeded to tell Steve the full story, He listened, yet never once tried to stop or interrupt her. When Isbel finished her story. 'Steve, I could not let you and your dad get involved. Burke would have used you to get to me.

Steve, then phoned Alex McCallum the Provost. Isbel sat there and listened as Steve ask Alex for his advice. Then placed the phone down. Steve did not say a word, but Isbel could see his brain working. After a brief moment, Steve phoned his father Ted. Isbel allowed Steve to have this conversation with him, when Steve finished with his dad, he turned to Isbel.

'Are you ready?'

Isbel nodded. 'Let's do it.'

The walk to Stewart Street Police Station took eight minutes, there was no conversation between them. Both of them with so much they were mauling over in their minds could not think of anything to say to each other. Steve worried that Isbel will be arrested and charged with the death of five persons, would be at least what could happen.

As they entered the Police Station, the Duty Sargent looked up seeing Isbel, smiled. 'We have been looking for you.' And promptly phoned a number. 'Hello Sir, Miss Jordan to see you…Okay, I will inform her. Would you kindly wait for a moment in the waiting room, someone will come and see you in a moment.'

The ten minutes wait felt like an hour. Steve sat there puzzled as to what had taken place, he had expected Isbel to have been taken into custody and charged straight away. Sitting there watching the police carrying on with their regular duties as if Isbel was no threat had Steve completely baffled. Even so, when a woman police officer asked them to follow her, he was a little disorientated with what was happening.

The WPC led them upstairs and showed them into the Chief Inspectors Office. 'Miss Jordan and Mr Blackman, Sir.'

The Chief Inspector William McCrea beckoned them to sit, as he welcomed them in. 'The Provost will be here in a moment, Tea, Coffee?' Isbel asked for tea, Steve declined.

Then a knock on the on the door, a smartly dressed man, tall of medium build, stepped into the office.

'Okay, Sir,'

'Jim step in… Miss Jordan…Mr Blackman this is DCI Jim Leader; Jim has been put in charge of this case, he will no doubt want to ask you a few questions about this awful mess we have found ourselves in. We have located DCI Burke's car at the scene of an explosion at the garage where your bother was murdered. We cannot determine the cause as of yet. But we believe that there are five fatal casualties.'

That was when the door opened, and Alex McCallum rushed in. 'Sorry, a few loose ends to tie up.' Then looking straight at Isbel. 'Isbel my love, what a tragic story this has all been. Many accusations have been said against you, but Interpol has cleared them up, with the backing of MI5. Of course, Jim here will need to verify a few queries with you, but mainly loose ends. You must be in need of some rest after such an ordeal?'

Then Alex turned to DCI Jim Leader. 'The reports from Interpol and the MI5 will be with you shortly, I suggest you read them first before interviewing Miss Jordan. Must dash another more urgent matter has arisen.' Shaking everyone's hands, Alex McCullum promptly turned and left them.

The Chief Inspector looked at DCI Leader. 'That's okay with you Jim?'

'Yes Sir, As you know I've just picked up this case, a little extra time would be most welcome to be able to come up to speed with this mess that Burke and Burn's has left us in.'

The Chief Inspector then turned his attention to Isbel. 'The state of your apartment, it is being attended to at this moment by the forensic team. Accommodation is being provided for you till it is ready. We can only offer our sincere apologies, for how this all came about. Of course, there will be a full inquiry into how our Officers conducted themselves. Please, in the meanwhile could you be so kind as to inform us of what compensation you may require?'

Steve kept a straight face, even through all that had been said, had squeezed Isbel's arm to make sure she did not respond also.

Isbel quiet response, led to the Chief Inspector to believe the distress Isbel was going through. But it was DCI Jim Leader that had Isbel's full attention. Isbel could tell Jim was a stickler for detail the way he held the folder and placed it on the desk, it was precisely the way he performed those simple task. DCI Leader was not one to allow even the smallest snippet of information go unnoticed.

The Chief Inspector handed her a letter, informing her of the Hotel that they the police were making available to her until her apartment was ready for her return.

'Miss Jordan, the way our Officers had behaved, I can only apologise. But DCI Leader will need your cooperation to establish what had taken place. So would you make yourself available to assist DCI Leader in this, so we can close this case as soon as we can?'

At Steve's gym, Isbel sat silently reflecting on what had happened, not knowing what had actually had transpired after expecting a much different outcome. That's when the phone rang, and Steve answered it. Isbel looked at Steve's face as he listened to the person on the other end of the phone. 'Alex McCallum.' Steve looked at Isbel, when he put the phone down. 'You must remain quiet, till Major Dupree, contacts you to explain the reasons why.'

Isbel started to realise that there were people out there that had another twist of fate for her, she also knew this would come at a price. These lifelines always came with covernant attached to them, the only relief she felt it was not the Americians that was watching her back, as she would expect a snipers bullet would be their calling card.

The Hotel was nice, better than Isbel expected. Isbel ran a bath with hot water. The soak in the bath gave her time to establish herself. Her thoughts, that could not leave her, was how DCI Jim Leader presented himself. It was not what he said, but more the way he spoke and handled himself that held her attention. He was not your usual run of the mill policeman, she had a feeling he would be someone, she should be concerned about. Good food and bed were high on her to do list. Thirty-five minutes later, Isbel decided she had soaked enough, and forced herself to rise from this den of iniquity she had pandered herself into. She took a warm shower to reduce the body heat she had built up in the bath. Choosing the black two-piece suit with a white cotton blouse, Isbel was ready to face the Restaurant for dinner. There were only a few diners there. She enjoyed the Barnsley lamb chop she had ordered for dinner, declined the dessert menu, ordered coffee instead. Tiredness started to creep in, and she headed for bed. The receptionist gave her a note as Isbel passed the reception desk, once she was in the lift opened it, to read that a flight to London had been booked for her. Schedule for a Ten am, take off. Agent Philips would pick her up at Eight am.

Chapter 13.

Thames House.

The Hotel's early alarm call had woken Isbel, now refreshed by making herself a coffee, with the espresso coffee machine that was there for the Hotel's guest personal use. Isbel was ready, a little overnight bag packed just in case. Clive was waiting as the lift doors opened, the beaming smile eased any concerns that she may have had, returned it with a smile of her own. A car was waiting outside, Luc was sitting at the wheel. The smile on his face, showing he was pleased to see her.

'Hi, Isbel.'

Isbel responded by placing her hand on his shoulder, just has she entered the vehicle.

The ride to the airport did not take long, and the talk was small talk. Clive, telling her that someone will be there on her arrival, to meet her and that would be Toni Buchet.

At the City Airport, as Isbel walked through the Arrival's lounge, Toni stood there, no sign was needed, just a big grin. Then with a kiss when they met. 'The Major wanted you to know, that you don't need to worry,' Toni confirmed this to her, when they were in the car heading towards London, from the City Airport. Crossing the bridge over the Thames. Isbel knew where the destination was the British Intelligence building, she had seen many times, on the News Channels.

Isbel was expected, was soon ushered into the building. The wood panelled room was spacious, as Isbel was led in. A large long table with many chairs was there, a woman dressed in a two-piece suit directed her to take a seat, then left the room. When the door opened Major Dupree, with several other people entered including Agent Freeman.

The woman that opened the meeting was Madelyn Sharpe, the head of British security. 'Miss Jordan, there are the good, with the bad things we find ourselves doing to protect the people. What you did was unspeakable to most peoples way of thinking. We are here to establish what it is that we must do to keep this Criminal fraction from taking control. If we are to keep a tight lid on this operation, we cannot allow a court case to jeopardise what we are trying to achieve here.' Then she allowed the spokesman for the CIA to speak.

'Miss Jordan, I know we have no proof what happened, what we do not know is how you could have achieved what you did on your own, we have strong believe that you did. We needed you to have handed over Jose Giraldo the Colombian, vital information could have been obtained that could have shut down these drug cartels.'

The head of British security with the most serious of looks, as she could to convey to Isbel. 'The fact that you didn't, but somehow you took, not just his life but the lives of Four others and in the way you did, this is what troubles us. Now our concerns will you be a threat to anyone else that upsets you?'

Isbel did not respond, as she was expecting more rebukes from them.

Major Dupree, nodded at Isbel. 'Their statements are asking you questions Isbel, would you like to answer them.'

Isbel directed her reply to the American contingent. 'Because of your lack of ability to apprehend this Colombian, you allowed him to be able to torture my brother Allister for four days resulting in his death.' Then Isbel turned and faced the woman in charge of British security. 'The police were also complicit with the villains, to cover up those of Allister's torturer's crimes, by implicating me. So my brother would never have had justice in your system, and I could have found myself in prison for a crime I did not commit.' Then turning back toward the Americans. 'And would you not have gunned me down like some mangy dog if you just thought it justified your needs? yet you worry how I will react.'

There was a moment of reflection from them, then Major Dupree spoke.

'The action that Isbel took, was in a convienent way to benefit ourselves, Isbel uncovered this collection of criminal organisations. That was setting up an establishment on British soil, that would have cost us all dearly, if it had not been uncovered when it was. Yes, Isbel's unprecedented response to the events that led up to it, had no moral compass in the eyes of the law. But in her eyes, there was no law there to help her to get justice for her twin brother and herself. Yet the help she gave us was priceless, that was carried out with much thought towards other peoples wellbeing. This is why I called this meeting, this was to clarify her position to allow her to live her life, and for us to pursue these villains, without us worrying about her. A lengthy court hearing could give the villains an upper hand with what she could give as evidence in her defence.'

Madelyn Sharpe was keeping tight faced, asked Isbel to leave the room so that they could discuss the matter in private. Isbel rose from her chair and made her way to the door. The woman that had shown her to the meeting room was now on hand to direct her to another place to stay while they discussed her future.

'Would you like a tea while you are waiting?' The woman asked

Isbel nodded and sat back to relax. Was she nervous? No. She felt quite calm she had achieved what she had set out to do. Now it was just to wait and take what comes, as it comes. The thoughts that kept coming to her, were now of Jake. That was all she had, that was on her mind. The threat to Jake had gone, for Jake needed not now, to be on the run. A smile broke on her face, Jake was like a sister now. The fact that Jake and Allister had been having sex together, almost made her a sister-in-law, Isbel liked that idea it pleased her a lot. The tea arrived with some biscuits. Though it did not stop Isbel from thinking, what pleased her more were the nice thought she was having. If this turns out favourably for her, what sort of life they could have together as sisters. Then the door opened, Major Dupree stood there.

'They have come to the decision that you will be left alone, no further action should be taken. A statement will be given to you, so that you know what to give to the police in your statement. This will be backed up by the MI5, with the aid of our goodselves the Interpol.'

'And the Americans?'

'Isbel, they are the American? Who are always reliable, to change their minds. Though they are all going to reimburse you, with the damage that Gordon Burns and Jose the Colombian, plus with the damage Burke and Burns did to your apartment ' Major Dupree touched her shoulder. 'When we take you to the airport you won't be travelling alone.'

Isbel nodded. 'Thank you, Major.'

'Take care Isbel.'

Toni Buchet was waiting outside with a car, to take her to the City Airport. As Isbel bent down to enter the vehicle, the smiling face she saw was Jake's. The reuniting of these two girls together, gave Toni a sense of pride, for Toni had like Jake's voice, it had a soothing effect on her. Now to see her reunited with Isbel, with the way they both greeted each other, made the conclusion of this case so worthwhile.

Jake could now tell Isbel of her secret. As they were sitting on the plane, Jake told Isbel that she had given birth to Allister's daughter before all this had happened. That her parents was helping Jake to care for the child, to look after her, till Jake and Allister, could sort themselves out to make a future for themselves.

***

Three weeks later, the funeral cars arrived at the Cemetery. The mourners were a mixture of Allister and Jake's friends and a small gathering of family. Denny and Lottie, could not miss this for Isbel. Nor could Steve and his father Ted Blackman with Alex McCullum. It was a solemn occasion as they stood around the graveside, with an arm around each other reflecting on their own memories of Allister. As the mourners started to leave, Jake was saying goodbye to them, Isbel was absent.

The lone figure standing on the periphery of the cemetery was straining his neck. He had lost his target, suddenly felt the barrel of a gun dig into the back of his head, Well that's what Isbel wanted him to believe, that her lipstick holder, was the barrel of a gun. 'You know the drill, and slowly does it.' The Agent found himself trussed up, the black nylon tie straps securing his hands, behind his back. Isbel now could check his identity. Her email to Jim at GCHQ giving a photo of this new American Agent. Then she sent the details to Javi. 'Your paymaster told you what would happen if I should catch you a second time?' Isbel placed the American Agents identity back in his pocket, then left him with the tie straps still securing his wrist.

Isbel rejoined the small group that was left, there was not going to be a wake. Jake felt it was not fitting to do so. 'Isbel it feels as I would be celebrating Allister's death, I just can't do it.' Jake had said, when the funeral was discussed between them.

Denny looked at Isbel. 'The Second one, in a week,'

'They are testing me, wanting me to strike out. Proving I'm a danger.'

'Don't you mind?'

'No Denny, I treat it as a game, like hide and seek. Jim Anderson loves sending details to Fairfax of their Agents, that are operating in Britain. He calls it his US postie game. Javi just likes the information, he believes it will gradually go away eventually.'

Lottie reached her hand out to Isbel and stepped closer to her. Arm in arm they started walking towards the car. 'When do you start back to work?'

'Five days time, Monday morning. I fly to Prague, to work on a spy film.'

All this time DCI Jim Leader had kept a sharp eye on who came, and made many mental notes. He had come with the Chief Inspector to represent Glasgow Police force. There was more to this case than what he was being told about, which intrigued him as to why would MI5, and Interpol give Isbel their full backing, also why the Chief Super wanted the case closed so quickly. The statements that they all gave looked good, actually too good, as all the I's were dotted, and the T's crossed, this fitted too precisely for DCI Jim Leader's liking. It was the incident in the garage that caused him to be suspicious. The forensic report could not come to any conclusion, as the heat that was generated from two forty gallon oil barrels exploding. These were the two barrels had had been filled with old used engine oil left there when the garage closed its doors, when it ceased trading. So when the fire took hold, the heat expanded the oil then it exploded. What evidence would have typically been found in a blaze of this description was scattered far and wide. The oil barrels were noted as being there when the forensic team investigated the death of Allister Jordan. Yes, it all sounded right. And yes it probably could have happened, as it was documented. But it was just too good to be true. Why did they not find any trace of Robert Burke's phone, that had been used to send the message to his father that he was in the garage? They had recovered the twisted burnt remains of DCI Burke and DS Burn's phones, and the sim cards and the phones memory gave them much information on the two officers activities. He also knew, that no new evidence meant he had no proof. But even if he had, would he be able to re-open the case?

The Chief Inspector was quite happy. The death of Burke and Burns meant that the threat of a corrupt police force inquiry had been buried. His reputation was intact, and he would not spend the rest of his career defending himself from those accusations.

Hugh McKeon managed to speak to Isbel during the funeral. 'The little bug has been crushed, and any infection from it eliminated, my regards to Allister.' He spoke in a solemn manner.

Isbel kissed him on the cheek. 'We have all done our best for Allister, which we should be proud of ourselves.'

The Christening of baby Alison, was as near to a name to Allister as Jake could name his daughter after him. Isbel was so proud to be the godmother for baby Alison. Denny had used many photograph to make a family Photo of Allister, with Jacklyn holding young Alison, as a family group; more for Alison when she grew older. Lottie had chosen the silver photo frame, using her sensitive touch. Which she called her fingers, her feeling eyes.

Chapter 14.

A Woman's Scorn.

Bucaramanga Charta Matanza in the jungle forest of Colombia set back from the main road, the front of the house looked normal. Hidden by trees and some smart horticultral architecture, lies the grand Hacienda Giraldo. Manuela Giraldo, the mother of Jose, sat grimed faced, staring at the picture of her son. The news of his death had just reached her, at first she could not believe what had happened. After reading the report three times. On how Jose had died, now it had started to sink in. Manuela did not shed any tears, they were for later, for now, she needed to have a clear head.

Manuela Giraldo had built this Cartel when her husband Emilio was gun down trying to protect his Boss Pablo Escobar, from the Colombian Police. Manuela had listened carefully to Emilio when explained to her how Escobar had built his Cartel, she had learnt that to keep what you have you must not let it go to your head. By making sure she had the right people around her (mainly those that had survived and had been apart of the Medellin Cartel) showing them respect, they would respect her and protect her. Jose was like his father, Manuela knew he was unstable, but had hoped that Gordon Burns would help her son to grow up, and show Jose just how capable he was of taking over running the cartel that Manuela had built up. Over time Manuela slowly had realised Jose would not be suitable, when it became apparent to her, that Jose had more influence over Gordon Burns. Manuela did not become the head of this Cartel by luck, she had built it carefully using her skill, off being one step ahead of her main rivals. Most of all not too upset the wrong people, by not looking a threat to anyone. Apart from those of her rivals.

Danna Giraldo, Manuela's thirty-five-year-old daughter, was now the obvious choice to take over. Danna's sixteen-year-old son, Gabriel, whom Danna had given birth, having been fathered by Gordon Burns, was being groomed to take over from his mother eventually. Now the three were sitting down discussing what will be the best plan of action, that needed to be taken, to revenge Jose and Gordon. The CIA report gave them all the information they needed. Manuela had one of the youngest, most educated operatives to infiltrate the Pentagon, so she knew what the Americain's were up to.

Silvia Bastoe at sixteen had been sent to Virginia, in America to finish her education. The plan was Silvia needed to attend a top University, then obtain a position at the Pentagon.

Silvia had singled out an American to marry, whom would give her American status. Silvia could not believe her luck how simple it was. She had worked hard and showed them how good she was by giving them much useful information on Manuela's opposition, the rewards for her hard work at University were to achieve top grades. With her knowledge of Colombia, the South America department at the Pentagon was where Silvia found herself. When she saw the report of how the administration had put the case against Isbel, with how they had believed Isbel had disposed of five victims. Silvia sent the report to Manuela.

Danna went through the details. 'We must not take this report lightly, if the CIA believe this woman was the one responsible, then we must take this as being the truth.'

Manuela nodded. 'Yes, I see by how they had profiled her, she was most capable.'

Manuela carried on reading the report, then looking at Gabriel. 'You have read this, and what are your conclusions?'

Gabriel, his eyes still looking at the report. 'If we are to take action to revenge my uncle and father, we must take care not to get it wrong.'

Danna looked at her son with much pride. 'Yes, you have seen what troubles us.'

'Yes, mother. Looking at the report, two things that we must take notice of, that I can see. First, how did she elude all of these special operatives that had all the training, snatch them from under their noses while they were watching the apartment? Secondly, she was clever enough and strong enough to take out Five people all much stronger than she was, in one go. Then to walk away from it without the British legal system taking any action against her. For I understand from reading in the report, she will not have to stand trial.'

'Good, you have looked at the problems that we must face before we make a decision. Let me stress the importance of what we could gain or lose on what action we take.' Manuela placed the report back in the folder. There was silence for a moment while they reflected on what had been said.

Danna was the first to speak. 'We would need a team that is specialised in this type of operation, who could infiltrate without being noticed.'

Manuela had closed her eyes, this needed time to access what was the best way forward. Her eyes opened when Gabriel spoke.

'The latest information in the report is that Isabel Jordan is in Prague. If we send a message to our Russian contact there, to keep an eye on her, to report to us on her activities. Would this not give us time to make the right plans for her demise?'

***

Isbel listened to Todd Baker very carefully, he was instructing Isbel on the way a handgun reacts when fired. 'Isbel, when you see car chases, as they are firing at each other. The chances of them hitting each other are quite rare, as the vehicle will be bouncing up and down and they will more probably hit a bystander than the person they were aiming for. Now I've chosen these guns, so you get to know how they feel when you fire them, From small calibre pistol, to a larger calibre pistol.' Todd opened the case showing the full range of handguns he had selected.

Isbel did not try to touch them but waited for Todd to show her.

'Now this one you must recognise, the Walther PPK 9mm. James Bond made this gun famous, with many of todays law officers, still prefer to use this gun.' Todd removed the empty magazine clip, then proceeded to placed three cartridges into it, then injected the clip into the firearm.

With the ear protectors on, Isbel took her stance, gripping the pistol firmly with both hands, she proceeded to fire the weapon as Todd had instructed her, let off the three rounds in quick concession at the target.

Todd looking at the target could see the spray as they hit the area. 'Not bad for your first attempt Isbel.' Taking control of the PPK, he replaced it back in the case. Then selected another. 'My choice of gun, the Glock 17.' Then he preceded to load it in the same way with three cartridges.

Isbel once more took aim and let of the three rounds. With Todd watching the pattern where they hit the target much the same as the PPK. Todd then selected the Remington R51 then the Berretta Storm followed by the Sig P938. 'This is the one the British military use'. Isbel had started to enjoy the experience. But when Todd introduced the 1968 Colt Commander 45 ACP, with its short Barrel length of 4.25'. Isbel understood what Todd had been saying as the recoil travelled up her arm. She had to steady herself before she took her second aim, then fired again. Todd explained why he had choosen this Colt to others. 'It is made with an alloy that reduses it weight, and being short it can be easily drawn from a shoulder holster, being less obtusive when carried in a shoulder holster. Though it is more unreliable in shooting on target over a long distance. At close range it is more affective than a 9mm.'

Erica had stood behind Isbel watching how she performed. 'That not bad Isbel, you have hit the target area with all that you attempted.' Then Erica stepped forward and selected the Berretta Storm. Loaded the gun than without hesitation fired five shots at the target, not one hitting the torso area. Placing the gun back in the case. She beckoned Isbel to look at where she aimed for. 'As you can see Isbel; arms, legs then the head. The first four to slow the target, the last to kill. Taking into account if the target was wearing body armour.'

Todd was always impressed with his wife's shooting capabilities with a handgun. His skill was more with a rifle. 'Let's give you the experience with dummy bullets.'

Isbel noticed the slight difference straight away not the same velocity in the kick, it was very small, but she had felt it. Then Todd wanted Isbel to fire a pistol, single handed with a live round.

'When we do the shoot tomorrow Isbel, you will understand what you must do to make it look authentic.'

Over dinner, the Stunt team went over the drill they would be performing the next day. Erica and Isbel were to be the doubles for the main stars of the film. Isbel loved performing, It was to her, the best bit of her work, also getting well paid for doing something she enjoyed doing, she was in heaven. Walking back with Erica to her quarters after dinner, Isbel sensed the feeling of being watched, she did not respond. She acted as natural as she could, glancing at window reflections, trying to catch a glimse to see who it was that was watching her. To Erica all was normal, that was what Isbel wanted. This tail was different from the usual American Agents that had been trailing her.

In her container accommadation, she set up her surveillance devices on her computer. The little pen cameras she had put place in set positions, so she could see what was happenning around the compound, when she had first arrived. Showed the lone figure, that now she could cleary see and identify. Sending a picture of him to Jim for his perusal. An hour later the result came back, that it was not an American Agent, it was a well known ex Russian FSB agent, who was probably working for others. This intrigued Isbel so sent a text to Denny for anything he could find out about him. Isbel did not seem to surprised that the reply came from Javi with an Egor Starikov details. And with whom he had been associated with. It was more of what he had been reported to be up to, in Prague, that Javi made sure that Isbel was aware of how dangerous Egor was.

Isbel laid in bed contemplating this new development, Yet could not understand why these Russians would be interested in her, she had no reference with them, to what had happened in Edinburgh, so why is this Russian having interest with her now. It swam around in her mind most of the night, niggling at her till she had, had enough. Slipping out of bed, Isbel dressed in all black clothes, then checked her computer it was a different person, yet at the same place, doing the same thing, watching her. Her quarters was one of an array of container cabins, like shipping containers one on top of each other. She had chosen this one for it had a skylight to it. It was her intention to have another means to escape if necessary, this was time to give it a try. It did not take her long as she laid flat on the roof and edged her way to the far end of the trailer then slipped down at the far end that was not noticeable from where the tail was waiting. She slipped amongst the other containers till she was behind the person that was watching. Then waited till she was satisfied he was settled. Her moves was carefully slow and steady, she knew she had the advantage of surprise. The strike with the training mitts, and her little bag of ballbearings was quick, the man was laid out on the ground, he had not known what had hit him. With cable ties securing his hand behind him, Isbel dragged him to a more secluded area of the compound. Checking that the security guards had complete their rounds first. She slapped his face to bring him around. His look as he recognised who was, that had hit him, was of a man knowing he was in trouble, not only with his captor, but those he was working for.

'Who are you, and why are you watching me?'

He did not speak, just stared at Isbel. The look from those black eyes unnerved him, the coldness that came from them, he was now acting with concern.

'You know I will inflict terrible pain on you, till you do speak.'

The man nodded, Isbel now knew he understood English. Isbel took a biro pen out from her jacket pocket. Taking the top off, she took a firm grip of his head and placed the pointed end into his nostril and began to slowly insert with a little pressure attached to it, as it slowly pushed up higher inside his nose he started to speak in an urgent blast. 'No please, I tell you.'

Isbel left the pen inside his nose. 'If you do not tell me everything, I will kick it the rest of the way up your nose.'

'Giraldo.' Just one word then nothing, he just stared at Isbel. Then he blurted out 'Giraldo, thats all I know.'

Walking behind the Russian, Isbel placed her knee into his back, then pulled his head backwards, to be able to remove the pen from his nose, then with her penknife she cut his ties. 'I ever see you again I will kill you, do you understand?' She stepped back from him, and as he started to get up, he turned, then lurched towards Isbel. She was ready, the kick caught him under the chin. As Isbel swung away to the man's left, was prepared to deliver the next attack. This was to his leg at the back of the man's right knee making him fall to the floor. Not staying still, she had positioned herself to strike again, the heel of her shoe smashing into his back, right between the shoulder blades, jarring his spin. He laid there in pain not being able to move, Isbel then smashed her heel down into the base of his skull. That was all she needed to do, her message to them that she knew.

The message Isbel sent Denny, Jim and Javi were just 'Giraldo?'

***

The Morning light shone through the window of the trailer, Isbel was already up and checking the surveillance cameras, Egor the Russian could be seen looking at the body of his sidekick. Isbel had been watching him for some time, waiting to see what he would do. He made two phone calls, then waited crouched down beside the body. Isbel checked her watch for the time, she did not want to be late. A van arrived, the Russian bundled the body into the truck. When Egor got in, the van drove off.

Then the first text came in from Javi. 'Emilio Giraldo died in a shoot-out with Colombian Police forces in 1993. He had been trying to protect Escobar. Jose Giraldo was his son. Will contact you when we find out more.' Jim Anderson's reply was much the same.

Isbel Jordan

The news that Danna received from Egor, Isbel had struck the first blow, that Isbel had taken out one of his trusted men. Did not upset her, Danna sat back in the chair, just took stock of what had happened. When she had revalued the information, it was then she relayed the news to her Mother, there was no reaction from Manuela, it was as if she knew it was possible it was going to happen. The two of them sat quietly for a moment contemplating. Manuela had made her mind up. 'Inform Egor to take her out.'

Egor received the message. This is what he hoped they would say.

Isbel sat in the chuck wagon eating breakfast, it was going to be a long day. These car chase stunts, took some time setting up, the Director needed to have as many camera angles as possible. Sometimes, one take is good enough, other times, four or five takes are required. But to Isbel, this was never like work, more like playtime too her. She had often reflected back to when she was young, there was no time for play then. This was catchup time. Todd had issued out real firearms, but blank rounds. Made sure all weapons were returned when the shoot was over. Erica and Isbel had enjoyed themselves, when back at the Chuckwagon, they all related back to how it had all gone.

But once that was all over, Isbels mind was on Egor, she was looking at how she would react if she were him, to finding one of his men had been taken out in that way. The smartphone that Denny had set up for her, could connect her to the computer. The cameras Isbel had situated to see all around the compound were showing everything was normal; that there was no activity, much to what she had been expecting. Working with Todd and

177

Erica, she had listened to all their stories. They had told her of all that related to how specific situation occurs, and how people react to them, because of the type of people they are.

Erica knew more then Todd on these type of operations, being ex CIA. 'We take extra care, not to get it wrong, a second time. As it don't look good on our records.'

Collecting some extra pillows, Isbel headed back to her trailer. Set the table up by the window. Fashioned the pillows into a dummy using some of her clothes, then placing one of her wigs on the head section, strapped the dummy to the chair. The chair was set back against the wall this would come into play later. Isbel.now took time to pondered about the plan that was in her head, till she was sure it was as it should be. Then laid out on her bed all her weapons that might be of assistance to her. The table lamp has to play it part, not to much light, only enough.

Nine that evening as the light was fading, Isbel saw the first movements on the computer. Two of Egor's operatives had positioned themselves, had started to set themselves up for the kill. Isbel could see that they had covered front and back of her trailer, the backup would be covering her entrance door, so it was the shot through the window of her trailer compartment would be the more likely be first, so carefully opened the window. She strapped a Commando Combat knife to her leg, then switched the table light on. Crouching down she pushed the dummy in the chair, towards the table that was visible through the now opened window, manipulating the fashioned arms of the dummy to look as if the dummy was her working at the table. The first shot came through the window, catching the dummy in the head, the wig spun off, then the second shot as the dummy was falling. Isbel in a crouching position, moved away from the table, moved as quick as she could to be able to crouch down by the side of her entrance door. Five minutes, the door handle moved, the door gently opened, the rifle with a silencer attached, poked through the door opening. As the assailent edged his way in through the door, the knife now in Isbel's hand lounged upwards into the top of the stomach just under the sturnum of the assailant, twisting it as it entered. The assailant fell forward onto the blade, pushing the knife, further into the hitmans heart. Isbel snatched the rifle, hurled herself towards the window close to the floor as she could, she had little time to act. She checked the rifle, and with one quick movement she pushed the end of the rifle out off the open window, aimed and fired two shots. The target laid still.

Erica was first to arrive, followed by two security guards. Isbel had already sent a text to Javi and explained what had happened, before contacting Erica.

The police had been called, but when they spoke with Isbel, they addressed Isbel as 'Interpol Agent Isabel Jordan'. Isbel liked what Javi had done for her. Reporting to the police, to what had happened, was now just a formality.

The phone call from Major Dupree, wanted Isbel to meet him in Paris in two day's time with the complete report on what had happened. 'Isbel, thank you for keeping in touch with Javi. We have a team in Prague at this moment, we have wanted Egor Starikov for some time now, you have made him show his hand, again my thanks.'

In the morning Erica made her way to Isbel's trailer. The look on her face was serious. 'We need to talk Isbel.'

Todd and Erica Baker were now concerned that this could have serious implications and needed to discuss this with Isbel and the Film Production Company. The outcome of the meeting, Isbel was being suspended until this had all blown over. Isbel agreed with their findings, for if any of the film crew had been injured she would have been responsible.

Egor was furious, the rage he was in, losing two more of his best men. But losing his reputation was what hurt him most. His phone call to Danna at the Cartel. 'I am sorry to say, that this woman has eluded us again, the cost to me is three of my best men, now the authorities are beating on my door at this very moment. I have to move my operation elsewhere; will be in touch.'

Egor was right without knowing. Agents Clive Philips and Luc Suttner with a very trustworthy group of Czech policemen, had moved into position. Four canisters of tear gas exploded as they were fired through the windows where Egor was hiding; the men inside did not put up any resistance. It was over in minutes.

***

In the morning, Isbel had packed her bags. Many came to wish her luck, no more than Todd and Erica.

'So you are not flying back to Scotland?'

'No Erica, I'm taking the train to Paris.'

Todd with a grin. 'I know you did not have much of a childhood, but Disneyland? I didn't know that was you.'

'No Todd, Though it could be something similar. I have to report to Major Dupree of Interpol, I hope to be able to put this behind us, so I can get on with my life?'

One of the stunt team drove her to the station, this in itself was something new. Another way to see Europe, but it would give Isbel a chance to type out the report for the Major. It will also give her time to think. Isbel purchaced a train ticket, for Mannheim in Germany. There she would have to purchase another ticket for Paris. The scene's she was witnessnessing through the train window, distracted her from putting to many thoughts into her head.

Annette was waiting at Paris Glare de Lyon for her. Over coffee and a burger at the nearby Le Train Bleu, they spent time catching up on what had been happening. But mostly on Jacklyn's baby photos.

The drive to the Chateau was still on girl talk. At the house, the Major was just as pleased to see her although he tried to be aloof, trying not to show it.

'Come straight through Isbel we have much to discuss.' Isbel handed him her Computer, so he could read her report. He gave her a folder on the Giraldo Family. They both sat in silence reading.

'Well Isbel, this is the reason why I wanted you to carry on being you. We have had many reports of a new Cartel in Colombia, had no idea who was behind it or where it was located. We had the Colombian Jose's first name, but not his surname, until the autopsy on Jose, confirmed he was the son of Emilio Giraldo.'

'So, I was like the bait on the hook to flush them out' Isbel did not seem upset on that revelation, she accepted it as if purchasing a ticket to ride a bus.

'Something like that Isbel, I had Clive and Luc as close to you as I could without them getting in the way.' Then the Major showed Isbel a series of photos, showing how Clive and Luc had tried to keep up with her. 'When Clive saw how you handled the first of Starikov's men, he did not want to interfere. Just waited and followed the van with Egor in it, so that how we knew where Egor had his base.'

Isbel did not get upset, nor react to what the Major had revealed to her, she just listened.

'When you gave Javi the information to what you had obtained from that first man. I knew I had calculated you right. Keeping GCHQ informed, have allowed MI6 to believe in you as well.'

The Major called for Javi. His smiling face said a lot to Isbel, then the kiss on the cheek from him. Isbel felt at home. Javi had introduced a folder, its content had many photos of a grand house and who owned the property.

'When we captured Egor, we aquired his phone. We were able to pinpoint where the last messages were situated, it indicated it was at this location in Colombia. We believe this is the Hacienda Giraldo. It looks normal until we put the microscope to it. Then we have this.' Javi showed some recently taken photos, of a large house in a well landscaped garden set-up, with numbered cicles to indicate where the other close up photo were protraying. 'Isbel, this gave us, a much clearer look. This made the reasoning why he believed this was the headquarters of the Giraldo Cartel. It was quite extensive for a traditional house in that area, Then there were the guards with their special cover to keep Satellite cameras from detecting them. 'With the help of Britain. France had launched a Satellite that orbits on a slightly different orbit than the American Satellite. This Satellite, have given us a different angle, for our cameras have good 3D capabilities.'

Isbel had already worked out where this was all leading, wanted the Major to commit himself. To go there on her own to a place she did not know, would be foolish. To go there with back up, now that would be different. Isbel remembered how she had felt when Allister died, can understand how the Giraldo family wanted the same as she did. There was nothing worse than a woman's scorn. The fact that Jose Giraldo had committed his act in the first place, not herself did not come into focus with the Giraldo's. Isbel knew it would not end until one of them, had eliminated one or the other.

Javi looked at the Major, he had done his bit. Now it was up to the Major.

The Major looking at Isbel hoping she would say something. Isbel raised her eyebrows as she looked back at the Major.

'Okay Isbel, what do you want to do?'

Isbel just looked at him. The Major had noticed there was no coldness in her eyes, but they where searching eyes, looking for guidance.

Major Dupree, had to be careful he could not condone what he was asking of Isbel a private citizen. He knew it could not solve all the problem of the drugs that were being distributed around Europe and the world. So, he had to be careful how he handled this request that he must not ask her, yet would love Isbel to accept his interest in disposing of this family.

'Let us sleep on this Isbel?'

Once in her room, that she was again, sharing with Annette. Isbel contacted Denny, she knew this was not going to stop. 'Denny I have a problem.' Isbel related to Denny what had happened. 'Denny, I love my job, if I do nothing. I cannot do my job.'

Denny smiled to himself, he knew Isbel had taken her revenge. That was all she wanted, it was not her, to carry on with any other form of vengeance, unless someone attacked her personally. But she had not seen these Giraldo's, so it had not stirred her into anger. Denny then with the thoughts of when he worked at the Doughnut GCHQ, he had worked with a SAS Major, whose son had died of a drug-related crime. The hatred the Major had of drug dealers could entice him to help Isbel. Denny did not wait, made the request for Major Adam Forrester's file, on his computer, while he was talking with Isbel.

'I think, I may have an answer for you Isbel. Major Adam Forrester, Ex SAS. He has according to his records, trained for jungle warfare. I'm sending a text to him now. Let you know how it's going. Both of our love, to you.'

Isbel acknowledged Denny and ended the call. Laying in bed, Annette had overheard the conversation.

'So you might take up the challenge Isbel?'

Isbel, turning towards Annette.

'It's not as simple as that Annette, Interpol cannot be party to this sort of thing with out proof. Yet I know if I want my life back to normal, I must contemplate the possibilities of having to eliminate the whole Giraldo family. That's a big ask from anybody, I'm not a President or Prime Minister with those responsibilities. Who can give an order, then sit back in an armchair waiting for someone else to do the dirty work? It will be me, a snotty nose kid from a Glasgow Council Estate.'

Annette laid back in her bed, she could hear the misgivings in Isbels voice. It had doubt written all over it, Annette was glad it was not her decision to take.'

***

For someone who had so much on her mind Isbel slept well, Annette could not sleep as easy, it troubled her more, as she just tossed and turned. So, in the morning to see Isbel moving around as if she had no cares in the world, utterly confounded her. Annette laid on her bed just watching Isbel as the memories of Isbel were flooding Annette's mind on those first days she had met Isbel. The sheer elegance how Isbel moved fascinated Annette, the legs that glided across the room, with the way Isbel's body flowed to the imaginary music in Isbel's head, making her ballet move's pleasingly mesmerising.

'Morning Isbel, did you sleep well?'

'Yes Annette, I did. The text from Denny this morning has made my mind up.'

With that Isbel went and showered, leaving Annette waiting for Isbel decision. Hearing Isbel singing was new to Annette, this was the first time she had heard Isbel sing. The soft Scottish Ballard, Annette had never heard before. Of a mother's worry about her son that was going into battle, bidding the piper to lead him back home save and well. Annette understood Isbel reason for singing that Ballard, for Isbel was that warrior going into battle, will the piper lead her back home?

At breakfast, Major Dupree sat with Isbel. 'Have you managed to put any thought to what we had spoken about, last night Isbel?'

'Yes Major, I spoke with Denny McKay. Denny has contacted a Major Adam Forrester. Major Forrester has agreed to speak with us of the record. It must not be recorded in any way.'

Major Dupree, willingly agreed to those terms. 'So, when can we talk?'

'Denny will be in contact with us, sometime this morning with a video link.'

The call from Denny came in at Ten-fifteen, Isbel and the Major. Took the call in Major Dupree's office.

Major Forrester came through like an old veteran. His approach of I've done it so many times before, so what's different this time, yet he had the experience to listen to what was being relayed to him. The questions that Adam asked, pleased Major Dupree. Who could be assured that Major Forrester took everything seriously? That he was aware, where the problems could be, relating to ways that they could overcome those issues. Adam was not gung-ho about anything he had read the detailed reports that Denny had shown him reguarding Isbel.

'Major Dupree, Denny McKay has given me the breakdown of Miss Jordans involvement, and her reasons why. How she operated with the little amount of training is remarkable.'

Adam had studied the report and had come to the decision that Isbel had acted in an excellent military fashion, she had done what was needed, yet had not crumbled under pressure. Someone he could stand-by with trust, that they would stand their ground, not turn and run away.

'Though I would still prefer to meet her and get to know her, before taking on this venture. The British Army has a jungle training camp in Belize. Major, I will see if they will let us join in with their training program. This will give Isbel an idea of how we will operate together. I have faith in Isbel to be fit. It's the trust we need to gain with each other that is more important.'

The video link over, Major Dupree asked Isbel what she felt about the meeting with Major Forrester.

Isbel nodded, she had that look of yeh he's okay. 'Major Dupree, Adam Forrester has this father figure about him, you know you already trust him because he has always been there, type of thing. Though, we have never met.'

Major Dupree, nodded. 'I know what you mean Isbel, my first Commanding officer, was just the same kind of person; you just followed them, as though they were the pied-piper. You might not have met them before, yet you feel you have known them for such a long time. That what is known as having trust in someone.'

The rest of the day Isbel was with the Interpol team, sat and discussed all the information they had on the Giraldo's. The call from Britain's Intelligence headquarters to Major Dupree, lasted an hour. Then the Major spoke with Isbel. 'You have clearance, Major Forrester has a big say according to what I have just heard from London. You had better pack your bags, Annette will drive you to meet the last Eurostar to London. Good luck Isbel.'

The look of admiration Isbel could see in Major Duprees face, gave her the feeling that he had respect for her as person. The nod from each other, was mutaul.

When the Eurostar arrived at St Pancross, Isbel collected her bags, walked along the platform towards Customs Control. She felt good in herself, full of self-confidence, there was a buoyant feel in her stride. There was bounce in her hair as she strode along the platform. The ticket collector and elderly chap, could not help but smile at her as he checked her ticket. The lean well dress man standing beside the Ticket Collector stepped forward.

'Miss Jordan? Mark Jefferies. Major Forrester asked me to take care of you.'

And promptly took her bag. 'This way please Miss. We have clearance with customs control.'

The Jaguar car that was waiting had a chauffeur. Mark placed the bags in the boot, as the chauffeur opened the passenger door for Isbel. The ride to Vauxhall Bridge took fifteen minutes.

'Babylon-on-Thames Miss, to the locals, or Legoland to others. Most of the personnel that work there, call it Thames House.'

As the Jag pulls up outside, Mark was soon out and collected Isbel's bags from the boot. 'This way Miss.' Led the way for Isbel, then once they were inside, Security acknowledged them, with Mark still leading the way. Isbel knew where she was going, she had been here before.

The lady that had looked after her then, stepped forward. 'Miss Jordan, nice to see you again. This way please.' It was an office Isbel was shown into this time.

The face of Major Forrester, Isbel recognised straight away. Although the sharp suit he was wearing did throw Isbel. 'Hello Major Forrester.'

'Adam will do nicely Isbel.' As the Major stepped forward to take Isbel's hand. 'You must be wondering why you are here?'

'Yes Adam, Interpol could not condone this, so how will the British Government condone it?'

'Isbel, the two of us will not win this war on our own. We will definietly need some help, so with the assistance of blindfolds. You are officially here for a telling off, to be warned that your conduct is to improve, or you will face a terrible reprimand from Her Majesty Government. Unofficially you will be given every assistance we can to help you on this assignment. With me as your guide, and advisor.'

Isbel did not expect what the Major had to say, at first just nodded.

'Good, I'm glad you have taken the government's warning, and treating it with the respect to how it was given to you.' The smile that Major Forrester was wearing was showing he was enjoying himself. 'That will be in our records if anybody should show an interest why you are here.'

Isbel now understood what was happening.

'Isbel we need to give you a new identity, that is another reason why you are here. You will have a military identity, with a rank equal to mine, so it does not look suspicious when you are with me on the training ground in Belize.'

'Won't this create a problem with the Americans, Adam?'

'This is what we are trying to avoid, they have not forgiven you for refusing to hand over Jose Giraldo. That goes for a few here as well, they believe you took the law unto yourself and that in itself, you should have been punished.'

Isbel had settled into the informal way Adam Forrester behaved, he was treating Isbel as an equal. Isbel could tell that Adam was one off those men that felt everyone had a job to do, that if everyone pulled together and just got on with the task, not worrying about rank or posturing, the work gets completed more efficiently.

'So Adam how do you see me?'

Adam looked straight at her, starting from her feet and slowly working up to her head. 'Capable. Efficient. You should also be carrying a public health warning though. So any young man, having any ideas when admiring you, that you could make them go weak at the knees.'

Isbel could see that Adam had also researched her. 'Capable and efficient, Adam I heard that banded about by others.'

'Isbel when I go on missions, I need all the information that my grubby little hands can attach themselves too. Your guardian angel Denny McKay, was and still is my guardian angel as well. So what he knows, I know. How you achieved to do what you did was not down to luck, it was more to do with adaptation. Just like when a hurdler has to adjust his feet to be able to meet the next hurdle. I like that type of person. So capable of achieving what they endeavour to do, using what little there is around themselves, so efficiently, with the most effective of outcome that they can obtain.'

Isbel's silly smile was confirmation that Adam did know her after all, that is how Isbel saw herself. She uses what there is to gain from whatever she needs, to use to her best advantage.

The photo for the new passport taken, and measurements for her uniform. Adam bid her farewell so Isbel could have a few days at home with Jake and baby Allison.

Chapter 15.

Closing the case.

The newly purchased old Georgian house set near the Erskine Bridge, was in need of renovation, situated between Milton and Old Kilpatrick on the slopes of the Clyde. Clydebank House lies in one and a half acres of land. Jake's parents had moved in to help Jake and to be near Alison the baby. With the coming and going of their family and friends. Isbel felt she should not inform them, of what peril she was putting herself into. She did not want them fretting and upsetting those few days she might have with them. Denny had not even told Lottie, he knew it would worry her. The Morning was fresh, as the chill air blew down the Clyde from the north, biting around Isbel face and played with her hair, the damp feel warning of some rain was expected. As she walked to the Audi A3 a little splatter of rain was felt, just a few drops nothing that would bother her. The Audi purred into life, kicking shingle up as it edged its way out of the drive, then following the road down, turning left towards Erskine Bridge on A82 heading for Glasgow.

The lean but dapper DCI Jim Leader, Stood by the window in his office at Stewart Street, Police Station. Looking out onto the street, the weather was overcast and scattered drops of rain making the pavement damp but not wet. He had come to terms with his new office, his fastidious sense of tidiness showing. There was not a file spread out on his desk, no misplaced pieces of crumpled paper on the floor. Jim Leader liked his office clean, even his progress board had to be tidy. Every little detail in its correct order; dates, times even the tiniest little thing that looked like nothing, still had to be catalogued and have its position on the board.

DS Gillian Fairbrother forty-two years old, with her broad features and Mousey, coloured hair that was pulled tight to her head and held back by an elastic band. Wearing a light grey, off the peg tailored suit. DCI Leader's new Detective Sergeant was studying the progress board that was on the wall. The Chief Inspector had emphasised that this was to be put to bed once and for all. This is not what DCI Leader was all about, he hated loose ends, to him, this was a dish of spaghetti, that had too many loose ends. Even with the reports on all the activities that the joint operations conducted by MI5, Interpol and the CIA had shown no proof that Miss Isabel Jordan had assassinated five persons, and severely assaulted another, did not mean that she could not have done the deed.

Gillian liked how Jim had organised the board. The A4 slips of paper were all typed out so could be read without mistakes. Each victim had every known bit of evidence attached to their individual report, Gillian did not need to ask a question it was all written there. The sequence of events that Jim Leader had placed in order of dates and places, stretched out along the progress board, placing where Isbel could have achieved the murder of five people, it was all conjecture on his behalf, as the question marks he had placed with them, being that all his findings were only of calculated theories.

Allister Jordan's death, with all that was perpetrated in the interrogation and torture inflicted towards him. The Coroner's report on how it was carried out and how long the ordeal lasted for. These were facts that could be backed up, he had no worries on that score.

Kenny Dalrymple. The assault on Kenny and Janet Nesmith in Duntocher. Jim had related how he approached Kenny for his side of the story. This did annoy Jim, for Kenny would not talk. When showing Kenny the picture of Isbel, it was how he shied back, the terror in his eyes telling Jim Leader, to who had attacked him. Kenny's silence did not give Jim the definite evidence that he needed to press charges. The look Kenny gave to Jim, was just how frightend Kenny was of Isbel.

It was the five deaths in the garage that made Jim, really interested. The forensics had given him no real evidence as the explosion had spread most of the evidence far and wide. The phone memories in Burke and Burn's phones had provided much detail on Burke and Burn's movements, that the service providers had given Jim; with the times and their positions, as an when, with where they had used their phones. The bodies had been burnt out of any recognition, It was the DNA that forensics had found, that gave them who had perished in the inferno at the garage.

'How did it go in Musselburgh, Gillian?'

'I checked the neighbours to the McKay's. Isbel's Audi, was seen on only two of the days. When she had arrived and when she left Musselburgh, but one neighbour had seen Isbel in Dunbar. Listening to you saying to look at the subject and their habits, I checked the Gyms in the area. A gym at Craighall is where she spent most of her time, talking to all those that used the Gym, Isbel spent her time working out. The days she was not there was when she was in France helping out Interpol to find

Jacklyn Kennedy. I tried to find out what vehicle she was using, but nobody recollected her having one. So drew a blank there.'

Jim took a deep breath, these stop ends were like doors slamming in his face. He moved a couple of papers from the board to place Gillian's evidence in their sequence of order.

'Does this get us any closer to the truth, Jim?'

'No, we will have to speak with Miss Jordan at some time, but at this moment we have nothing.'

Jim sat back in his chair and mauled over what he had; but the more he delved into it, the more he realised that the three Organisation, CIA, MI5 and Interpol had it well sown up.

The delivery of the Military Clothing, Air tickets and Passport informing Isbel that all was ready. The flight would take her to Barbados, a stopover for two days. Then change into the uniform, for the military plane to Belize. Then the text message from Denny informed her that a DS Fairbrother had been making inquiries around the neighbourhood and the Gym. Isbel had phoned Steve and spoke about what Denny had found out. Steve told her to see him the next morning, that would give him time to talk with his dad and Alex.

And that was where Isbel was heading. She drove into the car parking area at Steve's Gym, while waiting for a space to come available, she phoned Stewart Street to speak with DCI Leader. Sergeant Brodie who took the call. ' Aye, it will be nice to see you again Isbel.' In a jovial manner.

Entering the Gym, Steve greeted her with a hug and kisses on both her cheeks. 'You know they have nothing to go on, DCI Leader has been told to close the case, but according to Alex McCullum. Jim is a stickler for getting his facts right. He has a ninty-nine per cent success rate of a completion record. Be careful don't underestimate him.'

Isbel kissed Steve as she left and walked the distance to Stewart Street. The eight-minute walk gave Isbel time to reflect on the statement Major Dupree had given her, within a copy of the statement she had given the Police. Could she add anything more, so she settled on looking, as to though she was assisting them, in every way she could without wandering from what the Major had given her?

As she entered the Police Station, Sergeant Brodie was all smiles seeing her. 'You are a sight for sore eyes Isbel, even when you were younger, you never ceased to amaze me. Now seeing you all grown up, it has becomes a pleasure to see you.'

'Sergeant Brodie, I still carry bruises when you use to clip my ear. Then those terrible things you use to say to me, scarred me for life. The nightmares I still have, because of what you said you would do to me. Now you speak sweet nothings in my ear. Shame on you Sergeant.'

They both burst into laughter.

'Isbel, lovely to see you, my love. You are expected, if you go and sit in the waiting room someone will be down to see you.'

Gillian was soon there, she had been reading the reports, with the profile on Isbel, so was keen to see if they matched. 'Miss Jordan, I'm DS Gillian Fairbrother, could you follow me please.'

DCI Leader welcomed Isbel into his office. 'I was hoping we could talk Miss Jordan.'

Isbel was straight to the point. 'We did not have a chance to talk…as I was flying out to Prague for filming, so thought I should come and inform you as soon as I was home. When I had left, you had just picked up this case and would need time to get yourself up to speed with what had taken place. I too was confused as to what had taken place with the terrible outcome, with the consequence it had. Is there any way you could enlighten me on what actually happened.

Gillian expression of confusion was so noticeable, she had listened and read the report from DCI Leader on Miss Jordan, that she could come to only one conclusion. To hear Isbel ask, did they know what had happened, had made her wonder who was kidding who.

Jim Leader's, expression did not change. 'Isbel, I can call you Isbel?'

Isbel nodded. 'Yes Jim, please do.'

Gillian had never known someone so blatantly unabashed as Isbel, there was no shame or remorse in her attitude as if she believed, she was actually innocent. Gillian started to look at the files that Jim Leader had written on his theories, that Isbel Jordan had perpetrated her revenge with the five deaths in that garage. Only looking up at Jim Leader when he started to speak.

'Where were you staying, when all this took place Isbel? As there is no mention of this in your statement.'

'Yes, Jim that is subject to the Secrets Act I had to sign. MI5 does not want that Information disclosed. As you know, I worked in conjunction with MI5 and Interpol on this. They were most adamant that some of the evidence must remain Secret. Yet I must tell you what I can, as long as it's within the boundaries of those restrictions.

Jim made some notes, then looking up at Isbel.'I see you kept yourself fit during what was happening?'

Isbel with the same thoughtfulness, looking as if she was unaware to what had happened. 'If your twin brother had been brutally tortured and murdered, and the police were aiding and abetting those that had inflicted that pain towards your twin brother. Would that not make you angry and want to do something about it.' The way Isbel looked at Jim, with those cold eyes Jim could only look away, looked down at his notes. 'I had to let off my anger somewhere, the gym was the best place for it. With MI5, CIA and Interpol in close attendance, that did not give me any room to do anything else, but to kick my heel down at the gym.'

'But you did vent your anger out on someone…Kenny Dalrymple?'

'Yes, I admit that I questioned him in Edinburgh, that I roughed him up a little bit. But that's how we found out what was happening in Edinburgh, it's why we informed MI5. That was when I was told to back off or else.

Gillian's careful look towards Jim, who nodded back at her. 'Isbel we were talking about the attack in Glasgow?'

Isbel gave a vague look at Gillian. 'How was I supposed to have carried that out, I was still in France, on that date.'

Gillian checked the Interpol report, then slammed the file on the desk with frustration. The date tied up with the report. Major Dupree had protected Isbel.

'Whatever made you think I did that, have you any evidence that places me there. I know Burke would have loved to put me at any scene, of any crime, he even said I was drug running. MI5 showed me the circular, Burke had sent to all the police forces, stating just that.

DCI Leader was now as confused and complexed and getting more frustrated as was DS Fairbrother, as all the I's were dotted and all the T's crossed. He had only one way to go, and that was to close the case.

'Thank you Isbel for coming and helping us to finalise to what had happened.'

As they shook hands, Gillian could not help herself. 'Miss Jordan, this has made me believe in fairies again, as I always believed facts would speak for themselves. So much of this has unanswered questions, as if a ghost has been amongst us and done such horrendous evil, then vanished without a trace.'

Isbel knew how Gillian felt, held her hand just that bit longer. Isbel's eyes coldly looked into the DS's eyes. 'When I was fifteen, three eighteen-year-old men were involved…with myself, being the victim of rape. One of those men's father, had a big influence in manipulating the evidence to protect his son, at my expense. Saying how he could not understand how vital evidence went missing as if it vaporised into thin air. Maybe, those same ghosts are still here in this building, doing those same evils. Many have a name for those ghosts 'Closed eyes'. Only wanting to see the truth through their eyes only. Building cases more on fiction than facts, satisfying their hungry gut feelings, when on the table were a plate of evidence they could feed on. Fairies float about in wisp of fantasies, clouding the minds of many, so if we do not want our judgement to be overshadowed, we must take off those dark glasses to be able to see the truth in the facts. For if I was so intent on revenge would I not have involved Greer and Erskine, who were just as guilty with Robert Burke raping me?'

Isbel eyes were now focused on DCI Leader's eyes, the coldness in them was stabbing him like icicles. He saw the truth, it was written in the devil's contract between MI5, CIA the Interpol and Isbel Jordan. All of them getting what they wanted with the bonus of no conscience attached to it in the small print. 'I can assure you, Miss Jordan. I have the facts to close this case. You have helped gather up all the loose ends, we can now confidently say the case is now closed.'

DCI Leader and DS Fairbrother watched as Isbel walked out of Stewart Street Police Station from the Office window. Isbel was heading back to Steve's Gym. Both reflecting on how Isbel had conducted the meeting, all had different views, but Isbel had all the answers.

'So, that is it we just close the Case?'

Jim could feel the pent-up feelings of Gillian, but knew he felt no different than Gillian did. 'As Isbel so lyrically put it, we cannot keep open a case, based on gut feelings only. We must have evidence which we do not have. So, case closed.'

This is why Chief Inspector William McCrea wanted DCI Jim Leader on the case, for he would pursue all expects of the case, then when it was closed there would be no comebacks to lay at his door, even the nasty taste of Burke and Burns, would be a history he no longer would have to answer too.

The drive back to Clydebank House, Isbel thoughts was still thinking of Stewart Street. Had she said too much, Though did it really matter? Isbel knew, although the Police will have to close the case, it would not be completely closed for herself, there was still the matter of the Giraldo family. As she drove onto the shingle drive to Clydebank House, she cleared her head. The space by the south-facing side of the house had ample room for a triple garage. This was her dream to have a room for her Ballet and gym training that it could be built on top and over the triple garage, her sigh that it could only be looked at when her mission in Colombia is finalised. Then she sat there parked up contemplating those possibilities. The thoughts were when she came to view the property, Ross Hampton the estate agent had let Isbel stand for a moment to take it all in, as he described the history of the house.

'This is a Georgian Grade 2 listed property, it was built for Major Jefferies of the Scots Greys, in 1817 after returning home from the Battle of Waterloo.' Ross Hamilton had stated that though the house had not been lived in for many years, it had been well built and had not suffered from any neglect due to it. 'As you can see only a little bit of renovation is needed to bring it up to todays living standards, is all that it requires.

'So history will repeat itself.' Isbel thought to herself, thinking of her upcoming battle with the Giraldo's. Then looking at the double entrance doors, her thoughts were now pondering on if she returns, she will build the garage and her dream. As she focused on the house, it was when as Ross Hampton was about to open the large double doors, she thought on how cold the house looked. It was when she stepped inside the large double entrance doors and saw the semi-circular mahogany Staircase in the hallway, did the full realisation on how far she had come from that Glasgow Council estate.

Clydebank House had still much work to be done to it, as it had lain empty for many years. The Kennedy family were well into the work, the famly being builders they were able to take their time to get the right finish.

While Isbel was playing with Alison in her room with Jake, Isbel reminded Jake that she was off to work on Friday.

Jake drove Isbel to Glasgow Airport to see her off. 'Isbel I keep pinching myself to think we actually live in that house. Mum and Dad said that we must be thankful for Allister for what has happened, It was what Allister had to endure to allow this in the first place.'

Isbel wrapped Jake up in a big cuddle. 'This is all for Alison, Jake., For she is Allister daughter, it is what all of us must endeavour to do, is to give her the best chance to grow up. For me, if I can give you the opportunity to live a good happy life, then Alison will grow up being happy.'

'But what about you Isbel don't you matter in all of this, What do get out of it?'

'You Jake, I have gained a sister. What we have gone through together ties us as a family, with new friends to share together. That can't be bad can it?'

Jake reached up and kissed Isbel on the lips. 'No it not bad, for it sounds great Isbel. Allister would have loved that idea too. His love for you was always there Isbel, for he knew you were always protecting him, even though he was a big strapping lad. He knew you had his welfare at heart.'

The cuddle between them was of two people in need of some kind of love. Jake had always looked up at Isbel with a kind of wistfulness, that someday, when Isbel got to know about her and Allister, she would approve of their relationship. This was that approval.

Chapter 16.

Hacienda Giraldo.

Isbel observing the start of the decent down at Philip S. W. Goldson International Airport. Belize, she could see the lush green jungle canopy that spread out below, that she will have to learn how to tackle, if she was going to be able to carry out, what must be done. Knowing full well, that the end result was never going to end with a happy conclusion for everyone, it was going to end in bloodshed for one of them, that including herself. The touchdown was smooth, though it was the humidity that she felt the most; as when she had left the plane, it was that damp sticky feeling of the humid conditions, that was now making her clothes stick to her body. Isbel knew in a week it would feel normal. Passport control went through without any problems, then it was collecting her bags from the luggage escalator, collection point. The customs hall was next then making her way to the pickup point. Adam had sent her all the directions she would need with the passport.

'Lieutenant Jones?' The young corporal stood to attention. 'Would you come this way, please Ma'am. Your transport is waiting.' His instruction to meet a tall slim black-haired, female Officer. Became crystal clear as this was the only female that had military clothing, that fitted the criteria.

The Land Rover Defender 110 series, was a standard army issue; the driver was keen to make an impression. 'Make yourself comfortable, it's going to be a long drive Ma'am.'

The two men kept the conversation to what Isbel was going to find at the base. The general small talk mainly with any news from home, yet Isbel felt them watching everything she did. In a way, she found it quite flattering. Adam had warned her to be careful what she said.

The camp was just as the men had described. The corporal directed Isbel to the Commanding officer's office then departed. As Isbel entered, Adam was already there.

'How did you find it?'

Isbel nodded. 'Fine Sir.'

'It's Okay Isbel. This is Colonel Geoff Badcock we have known each other for years.'

Isbel shook his hand. 'Please to meet you, Colonel Badcock.'

The smile was huge. 'Same here Isbel, but when we are here together like this, call me Geoff, with any of the men Colonel.' Geoff nodded at Adam 'Isbel, as you can feel the humidity, it will take a few days to acclimatise. So, I will take you on a tour of the base and your quarters. Corporal Taylor has taken your bags to your quarters already. So, shall we?'

The Colonel rose from his chair, now Isbel could take a good measure of him, five nine in height, stocky proportions in his late fifties. About the same age as Adam. But Adam was slimmer.

The walking tour was of great help to Isbel, as she had never served in the armed forces, this seemed strange at first, though it did make a lot of sense. The training facilities were much like Isbel expected, was looking forward to having a workout as soon as possible. Stopped for a moment to take it all in. The Colonel would stop now again, to introduce Isbel to those he thought would be beneficial to her, as Lieutenant Janet Jones.

Isbel had known about the traditions of the British Army, that she now must abide to. Though it was much the same on the film sets, with every star having to get used to being called something else. Then with the small standing parts Isbel had done, had taught her how to stand to attention, more important how to salute, mainly with all the little British military traditions, that was making her perform the part of a British soldier. Knowing she was only playing the part; these soldiers were not acting, for them it is, a way of life. They were training to be able to do what, when the times come to perform their duties efficiently. And that is why Isbel was there, getting herself to do the same, with the same outcome to achieve her mission with complete efficiency.

Isbel was quick to shower and changed into the light combat clothes, that Adam had supplied her with. He did mention the reasons why she had been issued with so many items of clothing to combat the sweat, that she will no doubt suffer from. At the evening meal, Isbel met up with the Drill Sergeant. The way he spoke to Isbel, she soon gathered that many agents came here for this type of training, it did not take her that long to realise, that he also knew she had never served in any of the armed services. Then he reassured Isbel, it was to be kept strictly between themselves.

***

Morning found Isbel already up and running, she had seen an area around the compound, that could be used to do her exercise programme, without interfering with anybody else. Yet felt eyes on her all the same. The old kit bag full of sand, hung to a set height was ideal for her kicks. Then with her training mitts on, she was in her element; took no notice of the humidity that was building up.

At lunchtime, Adam came and sat with her. 'It looks like I've got some catching up to do, Isbel. I heard that your work ethic was strict, though watching you, I will have to dig deep, to find that bit extra, just to match up with you.'

The Drill Sergeant offered Isbel, to join him in some unarmed combat, during the afternoon. Isbel accepted his kind offer.

There was ten personnel in all, three of them females. The drill Sergeant showed them what he wanted them to do, teamed them in pairs. He asked Isbel to accompany him on the mat instructing her to attack himself, did not expect what happened next.

Isbel did what Sergeant Edwards asked of her to do. It was the speed at which Isbel applied it, that had him flummoxed. From the first hand that Isbel had led with, knowing that the drill Sergeant would take grip of, then use it to turn her, throwing her over his leading knee on to the mat. It was not what Isbel had in mind, it was the complete opposite, as Isbel's long legs had spun her body to counteract his move, then dragging the Sergeant over her body, her legs now had wrapped themselves around him. He was laid out on the mat with no chance to defend himself. Adam was watching with Geoff, as they looked on in disbelief. Sergeant Edwards picked himself up, then offered his hand in recognition of Isbel's skill. He was supposed to have counter-reacted to Isbel's expected moves, but did not get a chance. Then when Isbel's elbow came down where his windpipe was, yet did not follow through. For if she had, it would have been the end of him. Isbel knew what Sergeant Edwards was planning, just one of the moves that Todd and Erica had shown her. 'Watch, Listen and learn.'

That evening Adam, Geoff and Sergeant Edwards, sat with Isbel and listened to some of her stories doing her stunt work. Sergeant Edwards was a veteran; he had trained many top agents. Including Adam. Now he wanted to help Isbel for a different type of armed and unarmed combat. 'As you know Isbel, we have one of the best fighting units you can get, in the Gurkha Regiment. Tomorrow, our own Gurkha Sergeant Havilda Rai will be here. He will be honoured to help you.'

***

The emergence of this very friendly Gurkha at breakfast, Isbel felt a warming glow towards him. He was so lovely and polite, she wanted to cuddle him, not fear him.

Isbel was shown to a quiet place, so the two of them could work without prying eyes watching them

The smiling face of this diminutive man, seeing how tall Isbel was, showed how happy he was to offer his help to Isbel. 'You have noticed already that size does not matter, but it is how you use it. We are not big people, but our reputation makes us big. Like our Kukri, it is not a large weapon, but in our hand's…it's the biggest asset we could have.' Sergeant Rai showed Isbel his Kukri. 'The unique shape of the Kukri gives us many ways we can use it to our advantage.' Havilda then demonstrated with the help of some watermelons, various moves to how he could use the Kukri to be at its most effective. He found Isbel, an astute pupil, she not only listened, followed his instruction to every fine detail, that he had demonstrated to her. It was just not the weapon that Havilda wanted to indulge with her, but also the mindset, that must be used towards it.

By the end of the day, Havilda and Isbel were as one with each other. Adam now understood what Denny had told him about Isbel. 'Isbel is the best friend you could ever have. Also, the worst enemy to go against. For you do not know how she will react until it is too late, to do anything about it.'

That evening while Adam, Geoff and the two sergeants drank beer, they watched Isbel going through her training schedule. The Colonel just sat back and admired how Isbel just kept up the pace. 'I honestly must say, that watching her…I can only enjoy the grace of her movement, I must admit, if I was her enemy, I would be stiff with worry.'

Sergeant Edwards, smiled as he nodded. 'I thought that I had been consumed by an octopus, how quick those tentacles had wrapped around me, then the elbow was at my throat. I have never been caught out so emphatically as I was yesterday.'

Havilda agreed with him. 'Like how she consumes learning, she wraps herself around it till it is a part of her.'

Adam was all ears for he was going with her. When at first, he had been thinking of taking part with this, Isbel was going to need help. Now Adam was thinking differently. First, he had thought she would need time to adjust to the jungle environment, but he could see that was not the case. Yes, he could see her sweating, but showing signs of stopping, no way. For now, it would be himself not Isbel, that will certainly need the help.

'Sergeant Edwards. Seeing how Isbel can perform, I am going to need every bit of training from you. So, it is not me that is left trailing in her wake.'

In unison, the two Sergeants spoke. 'Yes, we will help you.'

Colonel Geoff Badcock patted Adam on the back. 'Good luck old chap.'

'Thanks, Geoff, I think I'm going to need it.'

***

The weeks flew past, so much was put into the training by them all. Adam with Sergeant Edwards bringing him up to fitness. Isbel, with Sergeant Rai using stealth not brute force. The time had come to enter the fray of the Colombian Jungle. Isbel now had new papers. She is a botanist from Kew Gardens looking for endangered species of floribunda, Adam being her guide.

Sergeant Rai presented Isbel with her own Kukri. 'You have earned this noble blade, treat it with the respect it deserves.'

***

The flight back to Barbados, then into Colombia held no problems, as they landed at Camilo Daza International Airport at C'ucuta. With the paperwork checked. A jeep was waiting for them with the wording 'Department of Forestry of Colombia' in Spanish was written on the side of the vehicle. The girl driver was a Colombian from the British Embassy. She drove them to an old warehouse. It housed a battered old Argentina built Chevrolet 400, that would not look out of place, where they were going, was waiting for them. Inside the boot of the car were supplies and traditional clothing to help disguise themselves, plus an array of small arms and a L115A3 sniper rifle fitted with a silencer.

The girl gave them maps and the latest information that she could give them on the Hacienda Giraldo. 'Return back to this warehouse when you have completed your consignment, you can contact me on this number, you know the drill? We will have samples and the right reports to match with your research, to back up your visit here. Good luck.' Then the girl left.

Isbel and Adam stayed till it was dark then drove off, Isbel at the wheel. Adam had folded the map, so he could concentrate on where they were heading. 'Avenida 10, straight ahead Isbel. We can pick up route 55, where we will head south.'

Avenida 10 was not like roads in Britain, bumpy but driveable, then the main Route 55. The Colombian drivers of the large trucks, like in most countries, like to drive at night, their bright, colourful lights beaming out like a fairground attraction, with their traditional music playing loud on their radios, just added to the festival atmosphere they produced.

Isbel and Adam had dressed in the clothes that had been left for them in the car. Regular sun-bleached denim jeans and jackets, bright coloured cotton shirts, battered Sunuva straw cowboy hat, with bandanas. Curtsies from the girl from the Embassy. The boots Isbel wore, were her own Builders Specials, but her normal size, with steel sole plates and steel toe protector inserts, she felt very comfortable. The music was local, so to blend in with their surroundings.

After three hours Adam took over the driving, the road was long with many turns due to the mountainous terrain of the Andes. When the sun started to appear, they looked for a spot to pull over and rest.

Adam built a small fire and made some coffee, while Isbel checked out the area. This helped to stretch her legs. Breakfast was of Empanadas and Apepas, local delicacies although the Apepas seemed a bit dry, were soon washed down with mugs of strong coffee. Looking at Isbel, Adam without really thinking. 'Isbel what drives you?'

Isbel collecting the remnants of the breakfast meal together. 'Survival, just to stay alive.'

The slight pause from Isbel, Adam did not try to say anything just waited, for he sensed that Isbel had not finished what she had to say.

'Adam when I was fifteen and was going to court to defend myself, the psychologist that examined me, he asked, did I believe in right or wrong? I answered if I felt that what I did would get me into trouble, then it would be wrong, everything else would be right. He then asked if I believed in God, I found that hard to answer. The psychologist just sat and waited, he wanted an answer, so after much deliberation I said. If God was there, he was not looking at me.'

'So, you don't believe in God?'

'No, that's not what I'm saying Adam. When I needed him, he was not there? I was on my own, that's when using my own way of reasoning, was how I defended myself.'

Adam acknowledged Isbel with a nod.

'Adam, how many times have the villains got away from justice, because of technicalities. Then ask yourself why are we here, doing what we are about to do. Was it because it is God's law, or of the morality to do what is right? But who judges, what is right? If it is God, then we can do whatever we want to do, for he says nothing. If it is about the Law of the land, then why are not the police doing what we are about to attempt to do? So, it's all down to our own moral thinking, of right or wrong.'

Adam did not reply, he could understand Isbel. With the simple logic that she used, just to get by in life. That logic had worked for her, as it set the course. By using that logic as a compass to guide herself.

They checked their bearings they had still a long way to go and soon they were heading south again, the area they needed to find was 'Berlin.' They would then leave Route 55 then head north-east on makeshift roads. A small town in the mountains where they could re-fuel and collect supplies. Isbel's Portuguese and Spanish helped them to get by without suspicion, then they pushed high up into the jungle, it was hard work and relentless, they still needed to keep away from the main towns. Cartels always had spy's looking out for anything suspicious. For two days, they had circled around and found a place to leave the car, high in the mountain jungle, hidden from any eyes. Now it was down to footwork. The trek through the Jungle was not as dense as expected, there was much undergrowth of the Buddleja Bullata, with many types of trees like the Crediela Montana and the Cashew nut trees, yet it did not need much hacking back with a machete. So, they made good time, with less effort.

It was nightfall when they found the Hacienda Giraldo. They found a spot that overlooked the grounds of the House. Where they settle in, with the help of assisted night vision glasses, so to make a detailed observation of how many guards; their habits, people in and out of the house, with the general routine procedures of the running order of life in the hacienda. They could see the fence was a double barrier fencing, with an eight-foot spacing between them, a thorny bush with red berry's growing inside the barrier. The cover for the guards to conceal them was a canopy of leaves that hung over a flimsy pagoda that straddled over the inner fence of the barrier. This giving the overall effect that it was a part of the jungle. When Manuela Giraldo walked the next day, in the landscaped part of the garden, with her daughter Danna and her grandson Gabriel. Isbel could see the family resemblance to Jose. Adam pointed out some key issue he was concerned with; a plan was gradually unfolding. Thirty metres away from the house, a Crediela Montana, a form of rubber plant tree, had a branch that spanned the two barrier fences, three guards were close near to the house. This will be where Isbel will drop down. She had a particular interest in how these three guards behaved, they had become complacent, were very relaxed in their duties. The kitchen door was the best way in, after that, it was all down to potluck. Isbel had taken a keen interest of a ladder, that had been laid down by the fence near the Kitchen. It was already agreed that Adam would stay where he was, and cover Isbel's escape route with the sniper rifle, complete with silencer. Adam did not believe the need to use firearms, if they wanted the Colombians and the Americans to think, that it was a local assassin that had perpetrated the killings.

Isbel being extra careful, so when she was happy with what she had seen, proceeded to the tree. That was about two in the morning, Isbel had noticed how smooth the bark of the tree was, used her belt around her ankles to hold her feet together, then with Adam's belt to be able wrap around the trunk. Was able to scale the tree without a struggle. When reaching the branch took care to check that all was as it needed to be, before making her way along the branch. As the branch thinned it lowered. Waiting for that right moment for the guard to be at the right position, Isbel dropped down the twenty-foot drop. Just like a cat, she landed on all fours. This was something she had practised for a stunt in one of the scenes for a film. She did not waste time as Isbel hit the ground, then in one movement, rolled towards her first victim rising up behind him. Isbel's free hand moved quickly up to his mouth, as the blade of the kukri sliced the hand that was on the trigger of the sub machine gun, then it was across the throat in one quick decisive move. The first guard sank to the floor. Ten long looping strides to the second guard, who had been more interested in the cigarette he was about to light. His look of surprise, seeing Isbel. Was too slow to react, was soon immobilised as the kukri sliced through the air and his throat. The third was still asleep in his chair never to wake, all three with their throats cut.

Adam could only watch how quick Isbel was, it was to how much she had learnt from Sergeant Rai. Then he saw Isbel double checked herself, that all was clear. Adam knew this was it; it was now all down to Isbel. As she entered the house by the side door.

As Isbel entered the kitchen, finding it was empty she still double checked where everything was, then her long legs carried her quietly across to the door that led into the main house. Gently she opened the door just a little so she could peer inside. A guard was asleep at the base of the stairs. Another guard was sitting sleeping upstairs on the balcony, that looked like a minstrel gallery. Opened the door just enough to give as clear of a sweep of the area. Now with purpose slow and silently moved, as she glided across the floor, the Kukri in her hand flashed again at the first guard. She had no time to stop, taking the stairs three treads at a stride, she had the second guard, leaving him in the sitting position as if he were still asleep. Now she looked towards the bedrooms. Isbel could tell how the guards had been positioned, to where the bedrooms that the Giraldo family were situated.

The first bedroom door she opened, seeing Gabriel turn in his sleep, it would be the last move he would make. Isbel had no regrets; they should have let bygones be bygones. Isbel checked for any noise before leaving the bedroom, then as quickly as before, she moved to the next bedroom door. The gentle way she opened the door, she could see in the large mirror on the opposite wall in the bedroom, Danna sitting upright, her back supported by many pillows in the large king-size bed, a blindfold was covering her eyes. Isbel did not give it a second thought, when the deed was done, she wiped the kukri blade on the bedcovers. Now for Jose's mother. Isbel took no chances,

Isbel Jordan

with a small pause to check for any sounds of movement. She then took the tentative paces to the next room. The gentle lever down on the handle as she opened the door slowly. The bed was straight in front of her, with the startled look of Manuela staring at Isbel, with the realisation, just who was there. Manuela snatched at the Berretta Storm by the side of her bed. As Isbel was rushing at her, Manuela tried to aim the gun, was too late. Isbel knocked the weapon from Manuela's grip with the kukri, the gun hitting the floor with a part of Manuela's hand still attached to it. The safety catch was still on the Berretta, and that had given Isbel more valuable seconds to react.

With Isbel's hand covering Manuela's mouth, to stop her screaming. Isbel sat down beside her, and in Spanish. 'You should have left me alone. What your son did to my brother, was unforgivable. For you to want to carry this feud on, means now you must all die. For it would just keep going on and on.' The movement with the kukri was quick.

Now Isbel had to leave, yet she made sure she had left nothing to chance. She checked for any sounds for movement before departing.Then as she entered the kitchen stopped to collect Candles. Isbel had already noticed that there were many candles littered about, choosing three large candles, placed them on the far end of the kitchen table, then lit them with the matches that were already there with the candles. Then the next stage was too open the oven doors, turning on all the taps of the Liquid-Gas, on the extensive oven range. Leaving the house by the side door, closing the door behind her for maximum impact, when the gas meets the naked flame.

Adam when he catches sight of her leaving the house, was soon checking for loose guards that could interfere with Isbel's escape.

Isbel, also at first on checking the area, before proceeding, collected the ladder she had noticed beforehand, that had been lying next to the fence under the canopy. Places it up against the barrier, then ascended to the top of the fence, sitting on top of the fence, pulled the ladder up behind her and then spanning the barriers with the ladder, she crawled across the space. She had just reached the other side when the explosion happened, as she dropped down the side of the fence in amongst the bushes, holding on to the ladder pulling it with her, using it to break her fall, so she did not damage herself, on the other side which had bushes scattered about in clumps. Isbel then raced to meet up with Adam.

Adam did not move, he waited till Isbel reached him, the nod he gave her, was of admiration to how she had accomplished her mission. He did not need to ask if it was successful, as Isbel would not have made her exit if it had not. Then they made their escape away from the scene. They did not look back, though they could hear shouting as they made their retreat into the jungle, making sure they did not cut their way through, so not leaving a distinct trail behind themselves.

The climb was a struggle getting up to the track, that would eventually allow them to arrive back to the old battered Chevy, that's when they finally looked back at the smoke that was rising out of the Jungle. The steady drive back to the main road for the two day it will take them back to the warehouse. Isbel related to Adam what she had done, on the next day of the drive.

'Any regrets Isbel?'

'No. It would not have stopped; I would have been looking over my shoulder wondering when. Todd and Erica summed it all up when they said, innocent bystanders could be hurt in the crossfire. And I could not let that happen. So, it had to be them.' Isbel settled herself in the passenger seat. Then looking out through the side window, there was no sign of remorse on her face as she said. 'No Adam, you must do unto them, that would do unto you.'

Adam was well aware of that saying, for he had used it himself justifying his own actions. But could he have done what Isbel had done? Well not in the same manner for most of his kills were with the help of lead bullets. Never had he clasped his hand around someone's mouth, then dragged the edge of a blade across their throats.

Isbel still looking out of the window. 'Adam, what I did yesterday, is for my tomorrows. For if I had not done what I've have done, there would be no tomorrows.'

***

The warehouse looked a welcoming sight as the car pulled in through the doors, after a few days of hard driving. Faithful to the girl from the Embassy, she was there waiting. She spread out on the bonnet of the Chevy, many documents.

'This is what you will need, these are the forms you will have to sign in your own handwriting to match the signatures in your passports. So, that you get clearance to take these samples out of the country.'

The Embassy had done their homework, and all the I's were dotted and the T's crossed. This was still a part of the cover that was needed for them not to be detected in any way.

After they both had changed back into the clothes, they had arrived dressed in, from Barbados. The girl from the Embassy drove them to the Airport.

The plane was heading for Barbados, then a connecting flight to Paris Charles de Gaulle Airport. Where Annette was waiting and would drive them to the Chateau on the outskirts of Paris. The smiling face of Major Dupree said it all, it was the hug he gave Isbel that meant much more to her. The Major knew this would not stop all the drugs being spread around the world, yet this would certainly disrupt one small part of it, slowing it down a little.

Javi was there to show them the results of what they had achieved.

'These are the Satellite pictures that we are receiving, showing the burnt out remains of the house. We just have to wait now, to see what happens next.'

Major Dupree spoke mainly to Adam knowing his concerns about the drug trafficking. 'The French and British Embassies in Colombo are coordinating with other Embassies there, to step up the pressure on the drug agencies to seek out other cartels and to eliminate them, we have made a start we just need to keep the pressure up, so we can have chance to win this war.'

Javi could now show more images as Military and Law Enforcement Officers close in to mop up the rest of the cartel members, as other pictures showed the snapshots of Isbel dropping down and disposing of the guards. But the angles did no show Isbel's face, looked as though it was a local that did the assassination. But the smoke from the fire, that stood out more than anything else.

'We are waiting for any other form of enquiries? Nothing as yet.' Major Dupree was so delighted how it had all gone. Reached over and shook Adam's hand. 'You made it all happen, Thank you.'

Adam just laughed. 'I was taken along for the ride. My god didn't I learn something. I first thought I would be going as an advisor. I went as a pupil.'

Annette who was sitting and listening. 'You have joined us all in appreciating the sheer masterclass of a true artist.' Then looking at Isbel. 'This ordinary snotty nose kid, from a Glasgow Council Estate.'

Isbel could only smile at her, for that is what had made her, like how she was. Isbel's thoughts 'You are what you are, so get on with it.'

At Fairfax, the first satellite pictures of the large fire that was showing up on the screen had Eduardo and Silvia studying the footage to discover what they could make out of the what had been there. Previous satellite recognisance was studied, both were placed together to get a clearer view. Silvia Bastoe was studying the satellite images for any evidence, of who had perpetrated the attack. The enlarged image of the perpetrator that had single-handed broken into the Hacienda Giraldo, then had put it to the torch, burning it to the ground. Had now disappeared into the Jungle, Silvia's boss Eduardo Lopes, pulled all the information on this as he could find. He wanted to know why it was such a big fire, as the previous satellite images had not shown how big this house really was. Until now. For this was what his department was set-up to be able to do, find any possibility of properties that could be a possible new Cartel headquarters.

'Silv, how did we miss this one?'

Silvia knew why, did not want to disclose her reasons. 'Well, it was cleverly disguised, Ed.' Pointing to the way the jungle canopy was used to hide the overall size of the Villa.

As Silvia kept her eyes on the photos, knew she would have to make some changes in her life. Thinking about what her husband had given her since their marriage, it had not been bad, he had treated her very well indeed. The smile that crept across Silvia's face was a sense of satisfaction, the friends they had made, then with the nice home they had built together was something she had valued strongly. It was the realisation that she had no longer the need to send any more secret messages, that now had come more to the fore. Of course, she would have to dispose of any evidence that could incriminate her. Silvia could not help but congratulate herself on how it was turning out, as she could now relax. For the debt to the Giraldo's had just evaporated with their demise. Silvia's mind was now on how she must portray herself, knowing she must dig as much dirt on her former employer as possible to look as though she is a good CIA operative, and worthy of recognition.

The messages coming through from Bogota started to ring bells in Ed Lopez's head. 'Giraldo?' He typed it into his search programme, the reply was instant. Bringing up the most recent of incidences with anyone with that name.

Jose Giraldo. He read the report. And sent for the latest information that Jesmond Freeman could have had.

Agent Freeman, picking up the message, connected to the satellite images of the Hacienda Giraldo. The smile on his face, as he watched Isbel carrying out the assassination of the Giraldo family. Jesmond could not say for sure it was Isbel, from the pictures that he could see, but knew it was Isbel anyway. For a moment, he just sat there mauling over what he knew, and what was the gains and losses. America had wanted Jose Giraldo because they required to find out the status of the Cartels that had sprung up after the death of Escobar. Isbel's action had upset his bosses, yet Jesmond had understood her reasons. Then he recalled Erica Baker telling him of the way Isbel believes that if the people cannot trust the authorities of their way of upholding the law, too only use it to suit themselves. Then they should not expect the people to obey the law. He did not share Isbel views, yet understood why she had said them. After all, Burke and Burns had used their position to their own advantage, with Isbel being the victim of their intent.

Jesmond did not answer straight away, sat there contemplating the report that he held in his hands, then sent. 'This is all the info I have on the Scotland file, could you keep me informed of any new developments with this, Ed?'

Jesmond had not committed himself. Then he texts Erica Baker. 'Is Isbel, okay?'

The reply he received; Jesmond had come to except. 'Isbel is in Paris with a Major Dupree.' The thought of how Major Dupree had protected Isbel after Glasgow, Jesmond knew how he looked after his own informants.

Knowing Isbel was no informant to nobody. Standing up and walking to the window, Jesmond was putting every bit of his memory together. From that first meeting with Isbel to the meeting at Thames House. Now he started to piece a few loose ends together, these loose ends intrigued him at the time, yet could not define their real meanings. Jesmond paced the floor; two names were now coming into the reckoning. Denny McKay and Jim Anderson. Jesmond had come to rely on their ability to gain information, did Isbel depend on them as well? Isbel was always one step ahead of everyone else, she would have had to know what was happening to act the way she did. No one had known then how capable she was until the three villains disappeared. But it was how they were taken. Who would have suspected a girl with no training to have been able to carry out that undertaking all by herself, then looking at the comment when he was with FBI Agent John Keats in the McKay residents in Musselburgh? The mention of a coiled spring now started to become more apparent to him. They should have picked up on that then.

Jesmond sat down again; he knew questions will be asked. That was just because the name Giraldo had come up, this was how Fairfax works. You do not ignore anything, if a name comes up, explore the reason why. There will be five different departments all asking why that name? And will ask other agencies, just so they know that their office is on the ball.

Jesmond cleared his desk. Then collected the file about the Scotland case. Pulled out his final report about Isbel to see if he could add any new evidence towards it. He put his thoughts to the profiler's report on Isbel. They had done a good job, the profile fitted Isbel to a T.

The call was expected, as Jesmond collected his files together headed for the meeting.

Jesmond passed a copy of his report around the table to all the attendees, then sat in his regular seat. The Director glanced at Jesmond's report, for he too had pulled a copy to study before he called the meeting. The American Embassies report, on all the bodies recovered, had their throats cut, that included the three members of the Giraldo family.

Then Eduardo Lopes gave his reasoning to what he had found. The history of the Giraldo family, With the way the Giraldo family had disguised their Headquarters to evade being detected from the satellite cameras. Watching over again the satellite images, so they could all comment on what had happened. Though the interest in who had committed the assassinations did not cause too much concern, as they were all agreeing that there was not enough detail to give them a named suspect. That it was possible, that a local was acting on his own. Jesmond agreed willingly with their conclusions.

Back in his office, Jesmond replaced the files into the filing cabinet, not before kissing the folder. 'Night, night Isbel.' Though he knew this would not be the last he would hear about her.

No sooner had Jesmond sat back at his desk, the knock on his door. The Director of Operations stepped in.

'Ah Jess, this is off the record.'

Stacey Burroughs; lean six feet, silver-haired, with much history working in the field. Pulled a chair and sat down. 'I took your demeanour of not saying too much at the meeting, that you believe there is more to this than Ed let on.'

Jesmond did not answer straight away, just looked at his boss; in some way he was expecting more from him. Then seeing the slight nod with raised eyebrows, knew his boss wanted an answer.

'Why did we not look at the Giraldo family, when we identified Jose? We knew he was associated with a cartel; did anyone check it out?'

Director Stacey Burroughs, with a gentle nodding action. 'I'm getting the implication that we were not on the ball.'

'Well, someone was not, or someone made sure we didn't.'

Stacey sat back and pondered that thought. 'Okay let's go down that track, how would they have achieved deceiving us?'

Jesmond had not thought about any angles on how it could have been done, he just had a little gut niggle. 'The way they disguised the building, someone must have given them guidance. It was good, too bloody good to have been by chance.'

'Jess, when I saw that twinkle in your eye, watching the perpetrator drop into the compound. I sensed that you might have known who it might have been?'

'I was putting some thought into how one person, could do so much on their own and not be a professional. The satellite picture does not show the full extent of how the assassinator was to be able to accomplish the drop from the tree without damaging themselves in the process. That needed some training to be able to execute that type of manoeuvre.'

Stacey's look, had a wry smile on it. 'Yes, your precise words, about that young girl in Scotland. If I should remember rightly.' The slight pause as Stacey looked at Jesmond. 'You know we put tails on her? It was not to know where she was, it was to see how capable she was. It proved she was, for every tail we put on her she tagged.'

Jesmond was not surprised at what his boss had revealed to him, Stacey had been around for a long time. He had pulled many hot coals out of the fire. He too used his gut feelings to prove theories as well as to execute them.

'So, Stacey, what is the plan of action?'

'Jess, I don't see Ed falling short on this, but it could be someone in his department who has leaked information.'

Stacey raised himself from his chair. 'Always nice talking to you Jess.'

Then Stacey Burroughs walked to the door, stopped turned then he smiled. 'Good looking girl, but not my type…I would worry about going out with the boys, thinking about what she might do to me when I got home?'

Stacey paused; his thought was now about future possibilities. 'Jess, keep her on your radar, she could come in useful.'

Agent Jesmond had already had thoughts, on the same lines as Stacey Burroughs, his operations Director. He was already working on the text he was sending Major Dupree on why Isbel was with him when the case against Isbel was supposed to be closed.

***

Clydebank House had started to take on a new meaning. Isbel stood by the taxi that had dropped her from Glasgow's Airport, looking at the work the Kennedy family had done restoring the house. The cold look had gone, but it was the happy faces from Jake and Allison standing by the tall window waving to her when seeing Isbel, that warmed Isbel more. A homecoming she had never received before, now made her feel very welcomed. This was born out when the smiling face of Jake's mother opened the double doors, spreading her arm to Isbel, a welcome that made her feel she was now home at last. That she had a family to come home to.

www.ingramcontent.com/pod-product-compliance
Lightning Source LLC
LaVergne TN
LVHW041701070526
838199LV00045B/1145